Stocking Feet

Stocking Feet

A Nowhere, CA Christmas Special

Dani Colman

with Chase Martin

For Dexter.

1945

1

It was early in the morning on Christmas Eve, and Alex Kaplan was monumentally bored.

He was polite enough to feel bad about it, at least. His parents were still asleep down the hall. They'd had a late night out in Santa Mira, with a fancy dinner in one of the restaurants that overlooked the ice rink in the square, and an evening movie. The movie hadn't been that good – some chintzy holiday comedy with stars who looked pretty great and acted pretty badly – but Alex had enjoyed himself nonetheless. It was nice to see his parents out and carefree, holding hands like lovestruck teenagers. It was nice to see his dad having a good time.

They had all come home well after midnight, and gone straight to bed. Alex knew his parents had fallen asleep almost straight away. His dad had taken up snoring since he had come home in

October, and he and Alex's mom – who had always snored – had kept up a repetitive counterpoint, not quite loud enough to keep Alex awake, but loud enough that he knew they were both completely dead to the world.

Alex, on the other hand, had taken a long time to fall asleep. It had been that way for months. No matter how late he stayed up or how tired he was from a busy day, he couldn't seem to fall asleep the way he used to. He'd lie in his bed long into the night, staring at the shadows of the trees outside as they flickered on his ceiling in the moonlight. When he did fall asleep, it would be fitful; sometimes strange, confusing dreams jolted him awake every couple of hours, but sometimes he just slept too lightly to dream at all.

Every morning, there he'd be, staring at his ceiling again, wondering what to do with himself until his parents and friends were up.

He hated to feel this way the day before Christmas, hated it particularly because he knew today would be boring enough on its own. At twelve, Alex was at that awkward age where he knew he ought to be helping out *somehow*, but none of the adults could find anything to do with him. There wasn't much left to do: his mother and grandmother would spend most of the day preparing Christmas dinner, but woe betide any man or boy who stepped into their kitchen while that was going on. His grandfather and uncle, always organised, had already chopped wood, dressed the tree, and hauled in the big table from the storage shed. They'd while away today hunting or fishing, and were unlikely to invite Alex along. He had never really enjoyed killing his own dinner.

That left his father, who liked to sit by the fire and read his books or listen to the radio. He had been that way since he'd come back: quiet, content, reluctant to move from his spot or change his routine. Sometimes Alex got the sense his father really did want to talk to him; he'd catch the green eyes he'd inherited flicking his way while he sat in the living room with his toys or his comic books, but he never quite knew how to start the conversation. If he was honest with himself, he was a little afraid to.

Eventually Alex decided that if the day was going to be dull anyway, he might as well get on with it. It had snowed overnight, and the cold hit him as soon as he pushed back the blanket. He retrieved his robe and slippers from under the blanket at the foot of the bed – a trick he'd learned at camp to keep his clothes warm during cold nights – and bundled himself up. There was just enough light outside that he didn't need to turn on his light: a grey, misty, predawn haze that made everything in his room shades of chilly blue.

To Alex's surprise, his dad was already up. Alex stopped short at the end of the hallway, the sight of his father in his green robe by the fire a momentary shock. Unsure what to do, he cleared his throat, and immediately regretted it.

"You're up early," his dad said, not looking up from his book.

"Yeah…" Alex said. "Couldn't sleep."

"Christmas morning jitters?"

"It's Christmas Eve, Dad."

His dad did look up at this, his green eyes strangely distant. "So it is," he said, "so it is."

Alex wasn't sure what to do with this, so he retrieved his comic book from the end table and went to sit cross-legged by the fire. It was a holiday issue; they were always silly, but he enjoyed them anyway. The silence grew between them, punctuated by the crackling of the fire.

"Hey Dad," Alex said finally, realising that he'd read the same page of the comic five times. "Can I look in my stocking?"

One present or the stocking on Christmas Eve. That had been tradition for as long as Alex could remember. He'd check the presents carefully, testing their weight, trying to identify one that would be worth opening early, but not the best of them – that was better saved for Christmas itself. If he couldn't find a present he was sure of, he'd go for the stocking instead: it always had some candy and enough small toys to occupy him for an afternoon, even if they were cheap things that usually broke within the day.

Alex's dad looked at him with that same slightly distant gaze. "Sure, son," he said.

Christmas Eve *afternoon*. That was when Alex got to open one early present. But he was already up and the day was already boring, so why not?

Alex's stocking was hung on the wall to the right of the fireplace (they'd tried right above it last year and ended up with the whole living room smelling of burnt wool). It was smaller than his parents', but stuffed fatter too. The red wool gave a little under his hand as he reached up to unhook it. Alex wondered if it had a rolled-up comic book inside – maybe one of the pulp serials his mother kept insisting he was still too young for.

Alex reached his hand into the stocking, feeling whatever was inside squish under his fingers like cool putty, and pulled out an entire foot.

He yelped, and flung it away like it was a live rat. The foot thumped across the carpet and came to rest in front of the fireplace. The skin was a waxy, hairless peach; the toes were perfectly-formed, like little blobs of wax on the outside of a candlestick. Five little toenails sat on top of the toes like half-moon slivers of glass. Where the ankle should have been, the top of the foot was cut cleanly off, pinkish and bloodless like a perfectly-sliced grapefruit.

"What's the matter, son?" Alex's dad asked, looking up at Alex with the same slight detachment. "Don't you like your stocking?"

"It's a *foot*, Dad!" Alex gasped.

"That's right," said Alex's dad.

"But it's…it's…it's a *foot*!"

Alex's dad looked at his son with calm, curious patience. "If you don't like it," he said, "you can put it back and open a present instead. I won't tell your mother. You just have to pretend to be surprised on Christmas Day, alright?"

Alex stared at his dad. The stocking was still limp in his hand, with something hard and knobbly weighing down the toe. For a surreal second Alex found himself wondering if there were a roasted chestnut or piece of hard candy in there. A good gobstopper could last him all day; it would be something small to focus on while…

He swallowed back a wave of revulsion as he suddenly made the connection that whatever was within the stocking had been smushed up into the toe by a *foot*. He dropped the stocking onto the carpet.

Alex's mom appeared in the doorway of the living room, rubbing her eyes. She must have been woken by his yelp of surprise.

"What's the matter, sweetie?" she said blearily.

For a second it seemed too absurd to say out loud (even though he'd already said it twice). But there it was, just in front of the fireplace, pink and perfect and completely out of place. "Mom," Alex said, his mouth so dry the word came out in a croak. "There was a *foot* in my stocking."

"Hmm," Alex's mom said, sweeping the room with her sleepy eyes until her gaze fell on the foot by the fireplace. She frowned and walked over to pick it up.

"Don't!" Alex cried, but she was already holding it. She examined it, looking at the five flawless toes with their little half-moon toenails.

"Don't you like it?" she said. "It looks perfectly fine to me. Is something wrong with it?"

Alex gaped. "It's…it's…"

He couldn't say "it's a *foot*" again. It was too weird. He walked over to his mom and took the foot from her, his stomach turning violently as he felt the smooth, waxy flesh beneath his fingers. He looked from his mom to his dad, and back again.

"It's fine," he said finally. "It's totally fine. May I make a phone call?"

2

Maureen was always up early. She was interested in birds, and the best time for birdsong was right at the crack of dawn. She picked up the phone on the third ring, and Alex told her what was going on.

"Are you *sure* it's a human foot?" she asked.

"I know what they look like, Maureen," Alex said. "I've got two of them."

"Three, now," Maureen said.

Alex called her a name he'd learned from a pulp magazine. Maureen laughed coolly.

"You want to bring it over?" she asked.

"What, my foot?"

"Sure, all three of them."

Alex had absolutely no desire even to see the foot again, much less pick it up, put it in a bag, and carry it all the way over to Maureen's house. Still, the only thing freaking him out more than the foot was his parents' strange calm about it, and it was worth spending a little more time with the disembodied foot just to get away from that.

"Okay," he said. "I'll be right over."

The foot was still on the end table where he had left it, which was odd: Alex's mom had a strict "no feet on *any* tables, *ever*" policy. Alex reached out for it, but couldn't quite make himself grab it. There was something about the feel of the cool flesh that made his stomach flip. It didn't feel quite like his own skin; it had a slight film to it, like bacon left to cool in its own fat. It was hairless as a baby's foot, but not nearly as fat and dimpled; in fact, it was pretty close in size and shape to his own. Alex wondered for a second whether trying to put a sock and shoe on it would make the whole thing more or less weird.

He very quickly decided on "more".

The stocking was still on the carpet, crumpled around the heavy lump in the toe. Alex picked it up and turned it inside-out, dropping the lump into his hand. It was a gobstopper, round and perfect with little dark flecks in the smooth blue sugar. Alex considered popping it in his mouth and using the familiar sweet taste to clear out the bitterness that covered his tongue at the thought of picking up the foot. That reminded him that the gobstopper had been in the stocking *with* the foot, and he quickly thought better of it. He tossed the gobstopper into the fireplace, where the fire flashed yellow for a second before settling into an orange halo around the melting candy.

Alex slipped the inside-out stocking on his hand, took the foot gingerly by the toe, and peeled the stocking off his hand and onto the foot. It was just long enough that he could grab the open end and pinch it shut without having to touch the foot itself. He glanced back into the living room. His mother had disappeared to the bathroom; he could hear the shower running faintly over the crackling of the fire. His father still sat in his chair, book open in his lap, quiet and content.

"I…uh…I'm going over to Maureen's, Dad," Alex said.

"Going to show off your present?" his dad asked, a flicker of genuine interest in his eyes.

Alex gulped. "Something like that."

Maureen lived in the good part of Nowhere. Not that Alex lived in the bad part, exactly, but there was definitely something down-home and cozy about the handful of ranch-style houses on Alex's block. They were, Alex thought as he placed the stockinged foot gingerly in the basket of his bike and started pedalling, exactly the kind of house you'd think of if you were describing a house as "okay".

Not so Maureen's part of town. Alex cycled the few blocks to Main Street, then turned left towards the lake. The town was still dark with early-morning haze, but strings of lights between the streetlamps twinkled colourfully through the gloom, giving it a cheery kind of glow. Most of the shops were closed and would stay that way through Christmas, but Alex spared a wave for Mr Gentry at the General Store, up early as always to make sure the truly habit-bound of Nowhere could still get a morning newspaper and pack of cigarettes.

Alex took another left where Main Street emptied into the road that circled Clear Lake. There was ice on the path, but nothing too bad, and Alex flew along the lake shore as the sky gradually lightened and the buildings to his left stretched and grew into generous lakefront houses with wide lawns. Maureen's house was at the neck of Buckingham Park, just before the lake shore kicked abruptly north into a peninsula. Maureen was already at the back gate when Alex arrived.

"Give it to me," she said without preamble. Alex nodded to the basket of his bicycle, and Maureen reached over the fence to grab the foot. She stripped off the stocking and held the foot up so she could see it against the cool morning light.

"Can we do this inside?" Alex asked. "It's cold out. My actual feet are going to drop off."

Maureen shrugged and opened the gate. Alex wheeled his bike along the neat path that meandered around the lawn while Maureen walked straight through the grass, still examining the foot as she went.

"Did it have a card or anything?" she asked suddenly, right as they reached the door.

Alex gave her a withering look.

"Oh, right," she said. "Because it was in the stocking."

"Because it's a *foot*," said Alex.

Maureen's bedroom was up the back stairs, on the second floor. Alex could hear the radio going from the living room, but Maureen didn't pay any mind to whether her parents were around. Alex knew they hosted an annual Christmas Eve party that everyone on Buckingham Peninsula and a few lucky souls from Nowhere proper were invited to attend. Alex and his mother had been once; she had put on her very best dress for the occasion. As best Alex could remember, she had spent most of the afternoon standing awkwardly by the bay windows while Alex and Maureen tried ineffectually to sneak out the back to play in the snow.

"You know," said Maureen, "when someone dies they'll put a tag on the toe. Are you sure the foot didn't have a tag on it? Maybe it fell off in the stocking?"

She stuck her hand down the stocking and felt around in the toe to check. Alex didn't bother to tell her he was sure there was no tag. She looked like she was having too much fun looking for it; besides, he was distracted by the sudden idea that the foot might belong to someone who was dead.

"Does it feel funny to you?" he asked. "The skin, I mean."

"Yes, but I can't quite put my finger on how."

Alex resisted pointing out that she had her entire hand on how: having failed to find a tag in the empty stocking, she had both hands on the foot again, holding it so close to her face Alex was worried she'd get a toe print on her glasses.

She flipped the foot over to peer at the sole, then over again to examine the top, where it had been cut off from whatever leg it had once been attached to. She looked up at Alex, her expression some-where between horror and absolute delight.

"It's perfectly cut," she said. "Look!"

She shoved the foot under Alex's nose, and he cringed back involuntarily. Maureen huffed ir-ritably at him. "Look," she said. "It's like someone sliced off the ankle then put a piece of film on top so nothing would come out and make a mess. Only there's no film, it's just…look at that! A perfect little artery. It should…"

Maureen turned the foot upside-down again and gave it a little shake. Nothing happened.

"See!" she said triumphantly. Alex honestly did not. "It's like jello in a perfect mould. Just held in there, waiting for something."

Maureen shoved the foot back at Alex and went hunting for something on her vanity, which was a mess of photographs and bird books and half a science kit. Alex held the foot by the very tips of his fingers as she searched, wishing desperately that she hadn't suggested whoever the foot belonged to was dead.

"A-hah!" Maureen pulled out a magnifying glass from between two trays of iridescent dead beetles. She came right over to Alex and peered through the glass at the top of the foot, pushing the whole business uncomfortably close to Alex's chest as she leaned in for the best possible angle. Alex felt his index finger slip in between two of the cool toes as he adjusted his position, and had to swallow back an unpleasant belch of disgust.

"See anything useful?" he asked.

Maureen looked up from the foot, her eye cartoonishly huge behind the magnifying glass and her glasses. "Nope," she said.

Alex seized the opportunity to hand the foot back to her. She set it carefully on the vanity, on top of one of her bird books.

"I wish I had a microscope," she said. "I could shear off a little piece and look at the cells. Then maybe I could…oh, wait a minute."

"What?" asked Alex.

Maureen grinned wickedly. "I just remembered I asked for one for Christmas," she said.

Before Alex could even start to say how much he hated the idea of cutting slices off the foot, Maureen was off downstairs, leaving him alone in the room with it.

3

It took Maureen about ten minutes to come back, ten minutes in which the sky grew a little lighter and Alex did his very best not to look at the foot on the vanity. When she returned, she was holding a big box, wrapped in striped red paper with a cheerful, gold-edged bow.

"I'm pretty sure this is it," she said, kicking the bedroom door closed with her heel.

"Your parents are letting you open it?" Alex asked. An entire microscope seemed to violate the "pick a mid-level gift" rule of opening a Christmas present early.

Maureen grinned at him. "They won't even notice it's gone," she said. "I'll wrap it back up when we're done and pretend I've no idea when I open it tomorrow."

The science kit had a pair of tweezers and a little knife, and Maureen used both to carefully peel back the tape holding the paper closed. She worked quickly and expertly, and Alex quickly realised she must have done this before. He thought back to his last birthday, to the look of shock on Maureen's mother's face when he had unwrapped the expensive-but-dull toy car she had given him to discover a rude little message on the passenger side door. He grinned, in spite of himself. Maureen was blunt and more interested in science than people, but she could be pretty cool.

The wrapping paper carefully pushed back, Maureen reached in to surgically extract the box from inside. She had guessed right: Alex could see the words "MICROSET" and "Microscope" printed on the black box in thick gold type, along with some numbers and other specifications he didn't understand. Maureen opened up the box and gave a low whistle through her teeth as she looked inside. The microscope itself was in the centre, neatly packaged between cardboard dividers; on either side, test tubes, glass slides, and specimen bottles were held in place with little loops of wire. Maureen ran her hands reverently over the microscope, muttering something about its magnification power and the clarity of its glass.

"Could we, uh…" Alex said, worried she'd slipped completely into a trance.

"Yes, of course!" Maureen said, and with a few careful twists of the wire she removed the microscope, a glass slide, and a couple of sharp tools from the box. She cleared a space on the vanity by dropping a couple of her bird books unceremoniously onto the floor, and laid out her tools, the foot watching over her from its perch a few inches away.

Alex peered over at what she was doing, curious in spite of himself. "Are you going to cut a piece off the foot?" he asked. "What are you going to look at – a toenail? A bit of skin? Part of the" – he gulped – "*inside*?"

Maureen snorted as she adjusted the microscope. "I have to set the thing up first, silly," she said. Alex decided to shut up and watch as Maureen delicately pulled something out of a specimen bottle with tweezers and laid it on a slide, twirling tiny knobs on the sides of the microscope to get it just so. He liked science in school well enough, but he wasn't fascinated by it the way Maureen was. He could follow instructions from the teacher and usually didn't set anything on fire, but he tended to leave class not feeling like he understood much more than when he'd entered.

Not so Maureen. She asked a thousand questions every class, and was an expert at twisting their teacher's face into that peculiar grimace that meant he was paid to educate them but didn't have to enjoy it. Alex had watched her play with her science kits before, reading comic books in her room while she carefully extended the wing of a dead beetle so she could look at it under her magnifying glass. He rarely understood more than half of what she was doing, but watching her reminded him of listening to his friend Michael play his violin, or watching the girls in dance class do their pirouettes. He enjoyed being around that kind of dedication, even if he had no patience for it himself.

Maureen let out a low grumble and sat back in her chair.

"What's up?" Alex said.

"I can't see anything," she said.

"What, like it's blurry?"

"No, like it's nothing at all."

"Have you taken the lens cap off?" That was something he had heard his uncles say to each other when they passed the camera around at family gatherings.

Maureen gave him a withering look. "This is a delicate piece of scientific equipment, Alex," she said. "There's no lens cap. There's a complex array of mirrors and lenses that have to be aligned just right in order to examine the microscopic mysteries of the universe. And I know what 'just right' looks like, and it's not letting me see any-thing." She pursed her lips for a moment, think-ing. "Maybe there's a protective film or something on the inside and I have to take it out first."

"Like a lens cap?"

"Shut up."

Maureen slipped her fingers between the arms that held the microscope to its little platform, and unscrewed the bottom lens. After a few seconds, it popped free. Something fell out of the microscope and rolled across the vanity, coming to rest next to the book with the foot on it. Maureen stared.

"Hey, Alex?" she said.

"Yeah?"

"Does that look like an eyeball to you?"

Alex heard shouting from downstairs. He recognised the sounds of Maureen's parents' voices, but couldn't make out what they were saying through Maureen's bedroom door. He considered opening it so he could eavesdrop properly, but decided against it. He didn't actually know if Maureen's parents knew he was here, and they sounded furious. He certainly did not want to get in the middle of the screaming match they were having with their daughter.

Maureen had spent way too long examining the eyeball, peering at it with her magnifying glass, lost in the opportunity to examine a real piece of human anatomy up close. Like the foot, it wasn't quite right: it was cool and slightly waxy, and – according to Maureen – was missing what should have been a messy tangle of nerves hanging off the back. Still, she said, it was definitely a real eyeball. Smooth and round as a marble, its brown iris and black pupil stared vacantly into the room. Under the magnifying glass's augmentation, Alex could see the individual muscle fibres that made up the iris, thin filaments of green knitted together with undulating waves of brown.

If it hadn't been totally disgusting, it would have been quite beautiful.

"It can't be a coincidence," Alex had said unsteadily. "Me getting a foot and you getting an eyeball."

"Yeah, but what a weird way to hide a body,"

Maureen had answered.

Alex had spluttered and coughed at the idea. "Hide a body?" he asked incredulously.

"Like murder. That's how gangsters used to do it, you know. Cut the body up into bits and hide them all around town."

Alex had read about that in his pulps: mob bosses in crime-riddled, black-and-white Chicago, or warring bootleggers in Prohibition San Francisco. It didn't make sense, though. "Why put them in Christmas presents, though?" he had asked. "And how'd they cut them up so clean?" The neat, bloodless foot and the glassy eyeball did not square at all with those lurid illustrations of bone saws and pincers.

"I need to run an experiment," Maureen had said abruptly, and before Alex could protest at the idea of cutting slivers off the foot or eyeball for examination, she had picked up the eyeball and left the room. Shortly after that, the shouting had begun.

Alex heard footsteps coming up the stairs, and a second later Maureen was back in the bedroom. She was white as a sheet, clutching the eyeball so tightly Alex was worried she would squish it.

"What happened?" he asked.

Maureen walked silently over to her vanity and sat. She looked at the eyeball in her hand for a moment, then placed it on the foot, resting it in the little hollow between the big toe and its neighbour. It was such a bizarre sight that Alex let out an involuntary giggle, but Maureen just sat and stared at it.

"Seriously, Maureen," Alex said, "what happened? What was the 'experiment'?"

Maureen took a deep breath. "The thing that stuck out to me," she said, "and I didn't even remember until after you said 'Christmas presents', is what you said about your mom and dad."

"What did I say?"

"That they acted like getting a foot in your stocking was normal. Like they'd put it there, even. And that's weird, right? Even if they were pulling some kind of joke…"

"That's not the kind of joke my dad would pull," Alex interrupted quietly.

"I *know*," Maureen said. "So I wanted to see if my parents were the same. If any parents in Nowhere *wouldn't* pull a joke at Christmas, it's mine. So I took the eyeball downstairs, and went to the living room, and turned off the radio, and…and I showed them."

"And they freaked out, right? I heard the shouting – it sounded like they went nuts."

Maureen looked up at him, her eyes behind their thick glasses suddenly just as strange and vacant as the eyeball resting gently on the foot.

"Not about the eyeball," she said hoarsely. "They were mad I'd opened the microscope early. Father went on and on and on about how trust is something you have to earn, and Mother just couldn't believe I'd be so terribly rude, but…they didn't say a thing about the eye."

Alex swallowed. "Something really weird is going on," he said.

"I know," answered Maureen. "What do we do?"

Amazingly, and with a sudden spread of warmth through his chest, Alex realised that he knew exactly what to do next. "We call the Liars' Club," he said.

4

Joe Feeney had started life in Nowhere as an outsider. Moving down from Seattle in the middle of the school year, he was a scrawny city kid in a rough and hearty rural town, with a father off at war and a mother who had never seemed to accept that she actually had a child. He had been shuttled between aunts and cousins for most of his childhood, often neglected and underfed, and with his scrawny build, thick glasses, and rabbity front teeth, he had been mercilessly bullied by every kid in Seattle who so much as smelled his existence. His mother had moved them to Nowhere on a desperate whim; Joe knew his father had come home to Seattle from the front to find some other family in their apartment and no forwarding address. Now they lived in a cheap kit house on the wrong side of Nowhere Station, ate mostly beans, and spent the time Joe wasn't in school staring sullenly at the walls with the radio on.

It was a depressing, boring existence, and Joe hated talking about it. So when he arrived in class for his first day at school and the teacher insisted he tell the other students about himself, he did the only thing that made sense at the time: he lied.

It started out small: just a few upgrades that made him sound more interesting than he was. His father went from an enlisted man to a Lieutenant; his mother from a waif to a poet. He borrowed anecdotes from the lives of the boys who had bullied him, and added subplots from comic books to keep things interesting. Around the time he started describing the crime family who had taken him in after he saved the family dog from drowning in the Puget sound, he realised the story had gotten away from him, but by then it was too late to stop.

Alex, Maureen, Richard, and Katharina were already close friends at that point. Alex and Richard were generally fairly popular and easygoing, but they both had a soft spot for nerds and outsiders, which was how they had ended up with four-eyed Maureen and shy Katharina in their orbit. As they watched Joe realise he was in over his head and struggle not to collapse under the weight of his tall tales – as they smelled the rising excitement of the kids who liked to pick weaker kids apart – they all concluded independently that Joe was one of them.

Maureen got to her feet first, direct and matter-of-fact as always. "My parents are spies for the Russian government," she said bluntly. "They taught me chemistry when I was five so I could put mind-control compounds in Clear Lake and put all of California under Soviet control."

"That's nothing," scoffed Richard, jumping to his feet and his full, premature-growth-spurt height. "When I was two, my dad put me in an underground fighting ring for babies. I won my first championship belt before I could talk."

"Oh yeah?" said Alex. "My dad's in a secret military program to create superheroes, and he punched Hitler in the *face*."

"Is zat so?" Katharina chimed in, deliberately exaggerating the accent she usually tried so hard to hide. "Mein father *is* Hitler!"

Thus the Liars' Club was born.

They met in the attic of the old cannery, where a steep shimmy up a back fire escape and a collection of abandoned furniture made for a private but surprisingly cozy Club headquarters. Maureen arrived first, after calling around to Richard and Katharina and filling them in. Joe didn't have a phone, so Alex biked over to pick him up. One by one, they clambered up the fire escape and took their places on the musty old chairs, everyone but Joe clutching an object and looking somewhere between terrified and exhilarated.

The eye was already set on the table when Alex and Joe arrived. There was an old brass candlestick that had been abandoned along with the cannery furniture, and Maureen had placed the eye delicately in the top of it, where it sat staring at the group like an unblinking searchlight.   Joe shuddered as he looked at it.

"Cripes, Alex, you weren't kidding," he said, taking a seat as far away from the eye as he could.

Alex shot Joe a withering look.   "I already showed you my foot," he said, and he took the foot out of its stocking and put it on the table next to the candlestick.

"Sure," said Joe, "but an eyeball's actually creepy. A foot's just gross."

Richard stood, unwrapping something from his coat and placing it on the table. It was the mate to Alex's foot, a perfect, waxy mirror image except for a pair of freckles right at the knuckle of the big toe. "It was in my roller skate," Richard said, looking like he was about to throw up. "I don't think I'm ever going to skate again."

"Why, don't want to start on the wrong foot?" Joe said. Alex punched him in the arm.

Katharina went next. She pinched the end of the thick shearling mitten she was holding, and gently pulled out a slim-fingered left hand. She placed it on the table with the other body parts, and went quickly back to her seat, dropping the mitten inertly onto her lap.

"Anyone need a hand?" Joe said. Alex punched him again.

Maureen took quick inventory of the body parts on the table. She was a little paler than normal, but she was the least disturbed by being close to the collection of disembodied parts. "Two feet, a hand, and an eye," she said, as though everyone in the Liars' Club wasn't completely fixated on all four already. "Joe, what do you have?"

"An empty tree, that's what," said Joe. "I told you, I don't think Mom gave Santa our new address. No bits of a dead guy for Christmas for me."

"A kid," Alex said, startling everyone. "I think it's a kid."

He had noticed how close in size his dis-embodied foot was to his real ones before, but it was only now, as he saw both feet together, that it really clicked. Whoever had once been attached to the feet couldn't have been older than twelve for a boy, maybe fourteen for a girl. It wasn't just the size, either: there was something about their shape, with the smooth arch and rounded toes, that told Alex they belonged to someone about his age.

The rest of the Liars' Club took a moment to let this sink in. Katharina let out a long, slow breath. "Someone has killed a kid?" she said.

"And sent us the body parts for Christmas?" Joe exclaimed. "No way! That is too weird."

"And it doesn't make sense," Maureen said matter-of-factly. "Why would a killer cut up the body?" She looked pointedly at Alex.

"Why should I know?" Alex asked, horrified.

"Because you read crime comics, you ninny," Richard said.

"Oh! Right. Uh…I mean, usually it's to make the body harder to find, but then…"

"…why put the body parts in *Christmas presents*?" Maureen finished. "That seems like the best way to guarantee they'll be found. So why else?"

Alex thought, mentally riffling through the pages of some of his pulp noirs. "To send a warning, sometimes?" he said. "But that doesn't make any sense either. I don't know what someone would be warning us about."

"Joe," said Richard, "are you running cigarettes for the mob again?"

"Nothin' but handcrafted Moroccan cigars, Dick," Joe said with a grin, and for a few minutes the body parts on the table went ignored as the Liars' Club fell into a familiar, comforting pattern of competitive tall tales.

"Perhaps," Katharina said quietly, "the warning is for our parents."

Everyone fell silent. Katharina had told plenty of good-natured lies about her parents, and maybe even a few truths as well. But there was a lot she didn't say, and no one in the Liars' Club had been brave or stupid enough to ask for details about just what, exactly, had caused her parents to leave Germany and come to the literal middle of Nowhere.

Maureen cleared her throat. "I don't think that's it, either," she said. "Katharina, did you show your parents the hand?"

Katharina shook her head. "I figured out which present it was in and came straight here," she said.

"Richard, what about your foot?"

"Not my parents," Richard said, "but my aunt and uncle saw it."

"And how did they react?"

Richard swallowed. "Like getting a foot in your roller skate is totally normal," he said. "They didn't even blink."

"Mine neither," said Alex.

"Exactly," said Maureen. "Mine only cared that I'd opened a present early, even when I was waving that eyeball in their faces. If it's a warning, shouldn't they have been scared? Or freaked out?"

"Or *anything*!" Alex said. "My dad's still a bit… you know. But my mom just picked it right up like it was nothing."

They all sat silent for a moment, letting it sink in. From the candlestick on the table, the eyeball seemed to be watching them. Alex thought for a second he saw the iris contract minutely, the pupil shrinking as a cloud passed outside and the light in the cannery attic brightened for a moment. He shuddered.

"I think," said Maureen slowly, "that there's something particular about these body parts."

Joe snorted. Maureen stared daggers at him. "What I mean is," she continued, "they aren't acting properly biological, and they seem to have some kind of soporific effect on the adults in the room. Maybe they aren't body parts at all, or maybe that's not the point of them. Maybe they're some kind of code, or even an attack…"

"Whoa, whoa!" Richard interrupted. "That whole bit about mind control was just for the Liars' Club, Maureen. You can't be serious."

Maureen looked at Richard with absolute sincerity. "We just came out of a war, Dick," she said. "The greatest conflict this planet has ever known."

She looked around at the others, with the air of someone letting them in on a deep, dark secret. "Nothing speeds the march of science like war, Liars," she said. "Agents of chaos come in more kinds than just guns and bombs. My father says we're already preparing to go to war with the Russians. And we know the Germans – sorry, Katharina – performed hideous experiments. Chemical weapons, psychological tricks, mind control: those German scientists – sorry, Katharina – might still be trying to mess with us and steal back our victory. How can we be sure this isn't some dastardly German plot – sorry, Katharina – to cloud the adults' minds so there'll be no one to defend us when the German invasion comes? Sorry, Katharina."

"*Geh Staub fressen,*" Katharina muttered.

"So what do we do?" Richard asked. "How do we stop it?"

Alex felt a pounding in his ears. This was all horrible – he was sitting in a dusty attic with two feet, a disembodied hand, and an *eyeball* – but something about hearing Maureen lay it all out like that had replaced his revulsion with something else: a sense of purpose. If he and the other Liars were the only people to have figured this out, they might be the only people in the world who could do something. It was time to act.

He got to his feet. "Maureen," he said. "Go get that microscope. You're going to analyse the body parts and figure out what's making the grownups act so weird. Everyone else" – he looked around at the others – "you're coming with me. We're going to find the rest."

5

Katharina ran the numbers as they hopped on their bicycles and started cycling into town. There were about eighty kids in Nowhere, depending on whether you counted the houses and ranches scattered up the side of the mountain. Katharina estimated they had around twelve body parts left to find, assuming the limbs weren't cut at the knees and elbows as well. It could have been worse: Alex was glad they were in a small town and not somewhere like Santa Mira or San Francisco. Still, he thought, that was a lot of presents to search.

"How old do you have to be for the mind control to start working?" Alex wondered aloud. "Can we rule out the older kids, or is it just the grownups?"

"My sister's sixteen and she thinks she's a grownup," Richard said.

"Did she see the foot?" Alex asked.

Richard shook his head. "Too busy doing her nails or something."

Alex frowned. "Well, we ought to figure it out.

If we can rule out anyone over fifteen or so, that cuts the number of places we gotta search by a third."

"Maybe more," Katharina said.

"How do you figure?" asked Richard.

"You said your aunt and uncle both had no reaction to the foot," Katharina said. "That means the mind control works on more than one adult at once. If you were trying to get a town under control, you'd want to get as many people at once as you could, right?"

"I have literally never considered that scenario, but sure," Joe said, his bony chin clunking painfully onto Alex's shoulder as he rode tandem on the back of Alex's bike.

"Then we don't need to find one body part per *child*," Katharina said. "Just one per *household*. That creates the greatest likelihood of affecting the entire town at one time."

"Learned that in Nazi school?" Joe asked.

"Second period every Tuesday," Katharina said, completely un-fazed.

"So where do we start?" Alex asked.

"About half our school lives in my neighbourhood," Richard said.

"And the other half's in mine," said Alex.

"Split up?" asked Katharina.

"Poor choice of words," said Joe.

They turned south onto Main Street, intending to

split up at the edge of downtown, but didn't get very far. Right as the wider streets of downtown Nowhere started splitting off into the tree-lined avenues of the residential areas, they heard an ear-splitting shriek coming from one of the houses. Alex, Richard, and Katharina slammed their bikes to a halt; Joe toppled right off Alex's bike and landed in a muddy snow drift.

"Body part?" Joe asked, wiping snow from the seat of his pants.

"Body part," the others agreed, and they turned their bikes towards the sound.

It didn't take them long to find what they were looking for. Just a few houses off Main Street, a persistent, keening wail was coming from the upper floor of a pretty blue house with white trim around the eaves. Alex and the others brought their bikes to a stop just in front of the driveway. They all had the same realisation at once: if another kid was traumatised by receiving a body part in a Christmas present, they could only make things worse by showing up and asking about it.

As they sat on their bikes, listening to the hysterical sobbing and wondering what to do about it, Alex saw the sun glint off something in a snow drift below the window. He hopped off his bike and clambered over the fence to take a look.

"You realise there's a gate right here?" Joe asked, letting the bike drop so he could come through and follow Alex. Alex ignored him. There, sitting in the snow in a shallow indent, was a perfect little ear, with two sparkling earrings clipped to the lobe.

Alex picked it up. Just like the feet, hand, and eyeball, it was a perfect, smooth peach, slightly waxy on the outside and pinkish like a grapefruit where it had been cut. The earrings gave it an unexpected weight, but the ear itself was light and paper-thin. At the top, where the auricle should have curved around in a broad arc, the ear tapered instead to a delicate, slightly rounded point, like the wing of a butterfly. Alex turned and held the ear up to the sky. In the pale morning light it glowed translucently pink, a delicate web of veins branching out just below the waxy skin. The earrings glittered with miniature rainbows.

"Okay," Alex said. "One down."

He went to put the ear in his pocket, but Richard stopped him. "What about the earrings?" he said.

"What about them?" Alex asked.

"They're really nice."

"I guess so?" Alex was a bit nonplussed; he'd never known Richard to care about jewellery (or even really clothes) before.

"Shouldn't we try to give them back?"

Alex laughed. "Come on," he said. "They got thrown out the window. Whoever found them doesn't care – they just wanted the ear gone."

"So we keep the ear. We were going to do that anyway. But we should give the earrings back."

Alex stared at his friend. Something about Richard's insistence didn't add up. Richard was generally an ethical guy – he'd give back a dollar if he saw someone had dropped it – but Alex didn't see the big deal about the earrings. They hadn't been dropped; they'd been *discarded*. Surely taking the ear and getting on their way was more important.

Behind him, Joe started to laugh. It started as a suppressed giggle, but didn't stay that way for long: within less than a minute, Joe was cackling so hard he had to support himself on the fence as his face went bright red and tears streamed down his face.

"What's wrong with you?" Katharina asked, somewhere between impatient and amused.

"Oh my God," Joe wheezed, slapping his thigh. "Oh my God. This is Emma Cagliostro's house."

"So?" Richard asked defensively.

Joe managed to get himself upright just long enough to point dramatically at Richard. "You're sweet on Emma Cagliostro!"

"Am not!" Richard protested, but his cheeks were crimson. Joe howled with laughter and doubled over again.

"Shut up!" Richard hissed. Katharina had started to giggle too, and now Alex was worried that they'd attract attention. He was pretty sure Joe was right about whose house it was, and Mr Cagliostro was well-known as an intimidating man.

"Fine!" Richard muttered, turning to Alex. "I heard Emma say she'd asked for earrings for Christmas, and she was really excited to get something pretty just for herself, and…and…"

Richard was so red in the cheeks Alex was worried he was going to start whistling like a tea kettle.   Behind him, Joe was still helpless with laughter, though he was at least trying to stifle it by shoving his own fist in his mouth.

"Go on, then," Alex said irritably, giving Richard the ear. He, Katharina, and Joe – still stifling his laughter – backed away to the other side of the fence. Richard scowled at them.

Setting his shoulders, and looking ready to bolt if Mr Cagliostro opened the door, Richard knock-ed.

The door opened. Emma's sister Juliet, fifteen years old and every inch the haughty teenager, looked down at Richard with an expression of utter disdain on her face.

"If you're here to see Emma, you're wasting your time," Juliet said. "She's been wigging out all morning. Opened one present and went completely batso."

"Show her the ear!" Alex hissed from behind the fence. Juliet peered over Richard's shoulder to see where the noise had come from, and Alex, Katharina and Joe ducked down out of sight.

When Alex dared look again, Richard was holding up the ear for Juliet to see. "I…uh…I think these are her earrings?" he said.

Juliet took the ear as though every pair of earrings came with their own ear attached. She looked at the earrings, holding them up to the light to examine them, then she looked back down at Richard with one eyebrow arched.

"They are totally *wasted* on her," she said, "but yes. These are Emma's earrings. I'll get her for you."

The whitewashed door clicked shut, and Richard stood there helplessly, the ear in his outstretched hand where Juliet had dropped it. Alex, Katharina, and Joe came out from behind the fence.

"So," said Joe, "is it all fifteen-year-olds who can be mind controlled, or just the really annoying ones?"

The door opened again, and everyone except Richard took a hasty step back. Emma Cagliostro stood on the threshold, still in her pretty blue nightgown and housecoat, her eyes red-rimmed and puffy.

"I don't want them!" she cried shrilly, seeing the earrings (and the ear) in Richard's hand. "Get that thing away from me!"

Joe cackled again, and Alex elbowed him in the ribs. Richard quickly unclipped the earrings from the ear, and gave them a quick polish on the clean hem of his shirt. He held them out to Emma and tucked his other hand, still holding the ear, safely behind his back.

"They're, uh…" Richard said, his voice uncharacteristically squeaky. "They're really nice earrings. I know how much you wanted them. I mean, I heard you say in school…"

Alex could see Richard's blush flame across the back of his neck. Joe and Katharina stifled their giggles – badly – and Alex had to fight to keep from laughing as well. Richard stood his ground as Emma looked at him, something close to sympathy in her puffy hazel eyes. She held out a trembling hand.

Richard squared his shoulders, and placed the earrings carefully in Emma's palm. As the light caught them, they blazed a rainbow of colours, refracting and refracting and refracting across the planes of Emma's face. She looked at Richard with something like admiration.

"Thank you," Emma breathed. "I really did want them."

Richard's fingers were still touching the tips of Emma's. He took a deep breath, meeting her clear hazel gaze. Alex, Katharina, and Joe all held their breath.

Richard held up the ear. "Can I take this?" he asked.

"Shut up," Richard muttered. They were walking their bikes back to Main Street, everyone except Richard using all their strength not to break down laughing again. As the clapboard houses gave way to the wood-framed shops and apartments of downtown, they slowed, their bikes crunching to a stop in the snow.

"So what now?" Katharina said. "We have one ear, and it's nine in the morning. I think we have to move faster than this."

Alex shrugged. "Same plan as before, I guess?" he said. "We split up and hit the parts of town with the most families. Maybe we'll get lucky again."

Richard pulled the ear out of his pocket and

looked at it, running his thumb over the finely-pointed auricle.   The lobe still had little dents where the earrings had been clipped on.

"Wait!" came a voice from behind them. The four kids turned: there, running down the avenue towards them, was Emma Cagliostro, her blue housecoat flapping behind her and flecks of snow flying about her ankles.   Richard hastily shoved the ear back in his pocket.

"Look," Emma said as she caught up to them, "I don't know what you're doing with ears and things. And I don't *want* to know," she said pointedly, as Joe opened his mouth to explain. "But I got on the phone to my friends, and I thought you'd want to know that Isobel Winter asked for a silk scarf for Christmas, and it came on an actual neck. She'd probably like it if you came and took that awful thing away."

"Gee, thanks," Alex said.   Emma shot him a withering look, and he shut his mouth. She turned her attention to Richard.

"It was a real nice thing you did," she said, "giving me back those earrings. Whatever you're trying with these pieces, I hope you manage it."

She stood on the tips of her toes to give Richard a kiss on the cheek. Then she was gone, running back up the avenue in her slippers and her flapping blue housecoat.

Richard's face went beet red. "Shut up," he said.

6

Isobel Winter was all too happy to get rid of the neck. She knew they were coming for it thanks to Emma, so she was standing at the door when they arrived and flung it right at Richard without waiting for him to brake. Richard – who was athletic enough for the football team but not a big fan of running full-speed at other boys his size – caught it neatly and showed it around.

The neck was more interesting in cross-section than the feet and other small parts had been. A neat slice of spine looked like an illustration from a science book at both ends, and when Richard held the neck up to the sky, they could see clear through the section of throat to daylight. The truncated veins and arteries were wider than their counterparts in the foot, and glowed a gelatinous red against the light with their contents somehow held perfectly in stasis.

"Ooh, I wonder what that feels like," Joe said, jabbing at one of the arteries.

"Yeah, let's *not* stick our fingers in it," Richard

said, tucking the neck safely under his arm like a football.

Isobel watched them with disgust. Alex tore his attention away from the neck and turned to her. "Thanks for this," he said. "Do you know anyone else who…"

"Sy Benson," Isobel said. "Emma told me to call around."

"Thanks," Alex said. He thought for a moment, then realised he had no idea where Sy Benson lived. In fact, he wasn't entirely sure who Sy Benson even was: most of the kids from Nowhere went to the same school, but there were a handful who didn't – new kids, boarding school kids, one or two extremely religious kids who learned their letters and arithmetic at home. He wasn't sure which category Sy fit into; in fact, he only had the vaguest impression of someone with very curly hair and a very prominent nose.

Isobel sighed with all the disdain an eleven-year-old in a floral housecoat could muster. "He's in the big red house on Buckingham Bluffs," she said.

"Oh," said all the Liars at once. Everyone knew the Red House: it had been abandoned for years before a new family snapped it up in a surprisingly canny pre-War investment. Now it was about half-abandoned, with the side that sat into the hill still a crumbling mess, but the side that faced the lake a surprisingly stylish wall of glass and blunt, exposed woodwork. No one knew all that much about the family who had made the Red House their project – except, it seemed, the kids who already knew Sy Benson.

"Okay," said Alex. "Uh…nice scarf." He had noticed that Isobel was indeed wearing a crisp new silk scarf, a jaunty print of horses and hedgerows at odds with the busy floral of her housecoat.

"It feels weird," Isobel said, her expression of disdain cracking a little. "My mom insisted I put it on after I opened it. It's like she didn't even…"

"Yeah, I know," Alex said sympathetically. "I got a foot."

The disgusted expression snapped back into place. "*Gross*," said Isobel.

"Yeah," said Alex. "I know."

It was a steep cycle up the side of the mountain to the Red House. After about a mile of tortured pedalling, Alex insisted that Joe get off his bike and walk alongside them. Getting up the incline was much easier without the weight of a second person on the back of his bike, but Alex still pedalled almost as slowly as Joe walked, and by the time the little group was at the front door of the Red House, everyone was red-faced and dripping with sweat.

They took a moment to cool off in the shade of the pines that lined the driveway. The Red House loomed above them, its timber front with its massive windows looking out over a break in the trees to a stunning view of the lake below. The low wall alongside the drive looked newly-built, and the red paint on the front timbers had not yet faded in the piercing California sun, but over to one side – tucked in among the trees that clung to the slope of the mountain – Alex could just see another wing of the house, bleached pink and sagging under the weight of its own rot. He had heard that the Bensons had been working on the house since they had bought it just before the War, inching backwards from the magnificent front as time and money permitted. In seven years, they had turned half of the Red House into a palace, while the other half continued to collapse into the mountainside.

As Alex looked up at the house, wiping dust-gritted sweat from his face, he thought he saw a boy's face peering down at them from one of the upstairs windows. He blinked, and the face was gone. A few moments later, the tall front door swung open, and Sy Benson (Alex assumed) was standing there, casual as could be in a blue sweater and pleated pants. His hair was just as outsized as Alex's vague impression of it; his nose, not nearly so much.

"What's happening, ladies and gents?" he asked, watching the Liars pant and smear away their sweat with no small amusement. "Isobel said you want something of mine."

They left their bikes in the driveway and followed Sy into the Red House. Light streamed in through the massive front windows, making the high-ceilinged front hall seem even bigger than it was. Alex stared around in open fascination. It was clear the Bensons had poured all they had into remaking the structure of the house itself (half of it, at least): the furniture, sturdy but shabby, looked small and dingy next to the broad windows and towering timbers. It was such an odd way to come at a house, especially one that people lived in. Alex found himself wondering why the Bensons had decided to do it.

"I've heard of you guys, you know," Sy said, leading the group through the front hall and up a staircase. "That teacher you traumatised plays chess with my father. You're legendary around here."

"Really?" asked Joe, who had never been legendary anywhere.

Sy grinned, mischievous and admiring. "Oh yeah," he said. "Made me wish I had the chutzpah to pull something like that."

"Did you?" asked Richard.

"Oh, no," said Sy. "Mess with the teachers a-round here, you get sent home. Mess with them at Douglas Pine Academy, you get toilet duty for a week."

So that was why Alex couldn't remember interacting with Sy since the Bensons had moved to town. He was a boarding school kid: one of the handful in Nowhere whose parents were willing to pay good money for a quality education elsewhere and some peace and quiet at home. Alex wondered if Sy's school bills were the reason the repairs on the Red House were moving so slowly.

Sy's bedroom was also at the front of the house, off a little mezzanine that looked down onto the airy front hall. Sunlight streamed in through tall windows, Douglas pines stretching down the hill in front of them to an expansive view of the glistening lake. Alex sucked in his breath through his teeth. "I thought Maureen's view was good," he said.

Sy grinned. "I've seen worse," he said.

The torso was on a box by the window, a toy rifle strapped across its chest. Sy unbuckled the rifle and laid it against the wall. "Shame," he said. "I thought that was part of the present."

"Really?" asked Alex. "You thought getting a human chest was normal?"

Sy shrugged. "Sure," he said, "for storing the rifle or pressing shirts. Or maybe a punching bag – I did tell my uncle I wanted to join the boxing club this year."

The Liars looked at each other. "How old are you?" Katharina asked Sy.

"Twelve next month," Sy said. "Why?"

"No reason," Katharina said.

The Liars were quiet as Sy led them downstairs, Alex struggling a little to get a good grip on the torso. Sy offered to give them a tour of the house, and they were genuinely tempted. Alex wanted to see what was in the rotting, pink-bleached wing crumbling into the side of the mountain.

But it was more important to get to Maureen. If kids Sy's age – *their* age – could be affected by the mind control, they were in more danger than they had thought. With a sample as big as the torso, Alex was sure Maureen could figure it out, but they had limited time. First thing in the morning on Christmas Day, anyone they hadn't reached would be opening presents, and putting adults *and* children under the thrall of whatever was in these mysterious body parts.

Alex paused at the front door, adjusting his grip on the torso. Something about the Red House was setting him on edge, and he couldn't put his finger on what. It wasn't just the shabby furniture or the knowledge that the rotting wing was hidden behind all the glass-walled splendour, and it wasn't Sy's disturbing casualness about getting part of a body for Christmas.

"Hey, where's your tree?" Joe said suddenly.

All at once, it clicked. The Red House was the only place in Nowhere that wasn't decorated for Christmas. There was a string of lights over the fireplace, but that was it: no tree, no stockings, no gaudy paper chains or holiday knick-knacks. It could have been any other Monday in winter in the Red House's spacious hall.

"Didn't you know?" Sy said. "We're Jewish." He looked sidelong at Katharina. "No hard feelings, of course."

"*Entschuldigung?*" Katharina muttered, going bright red.

"I've got a couple of Methodist cousins who insist on sending Christmas presents – they even pretend they're from Santa, for Pete's sake – but aside from that, we stick to Hanukkah. Happy Hanukkah, by the way."

"*Mazel tov,*" Katharina said grumpily, and marched out the door.

7

They decided to stop at the General Store and get a bag for the body parts. The torso didn't fit in any of their bicycles' front baskets, so Richard had to ride with it tucked awkwardly under one arm. Alex didn't see how they could pick up anything larger than another ear and still be able to carry everything.

Richard and Katharina waited outside with the bikes while Alex and Joe went in. Downtown Nowhere was always sleepy on Christmas Eve, but a few other people were out and about, running last-minute errands or just enjoying a walk in the pale winter sunshine.

Mr Gentry happily gave the boys an old flour sack and some string to tie it to their handlebars. He also slipped each of them a piece of peanut brittle, not from the jar he kept on the counter, but from the box Mrs Gentry always sent with him to work in the week leading up to Christmas. Alex and Joe took the candy gratefully, only just realising that they had been on their strange quest since sunup without actually stopping for breakfast.

As they turned to head back out, they heard the bell on the door jingle. Joe turned to look before Alex, and Alex almost dropped the peanut brittle as Joe grabbed him by the sleeve and jerked him behind a row of shelves.

"What the hell, Joe?" Alex exclaimed.

"Shh," Joe hissed. "It's my *mom*."

Alex swore under his breath. Lisbeth Feeney didn't leave the house on the other side of Nowhere Station if she could avoid it. When she did, it usually meant bad news.

"I know you're in here, Joe," he heard Lisbeth say. Her voice always had a peculiar fullness to it; not the pregnant slurring of someone who was drunk or on tranquillisers, but a sort of weariness so thick it made words sound heavy coming out of her mouth. It made Alex uneasy to hear it. He knew Joe hated it too.

"Where are you, you little brat?" The fullness took on a sharp edge. Alex felt Joe stiffen next to him. He heard Mr Gentry breathe in sharply, probably to reprimand Lisbeth, but before he could say anything Joe stepped out from behind the shelving.

"What is it, Mom?" he said sullenly.

Lisbeth Feeney sized up her son. She had the same bright red hair and rabbity teeth as Joe, but the resemblance was otherwise not strong. Joe was scrawny but he had a wiry strength to him, like a coiled string with a round face and easy grin. Lisbeth was long and lanky, like wet string somehow knotted into a person. She looked, Alex thought, like what would happen if someone sucked all the air out of Joe, stretched him out, and put him in a dress.

"*He* found you," Lisbeth said acidly.

"Who?" said Joe.

Lisbeth looked at Joe with her pallid grey eyes. The harshness in her voice didn't reach her gaze; Alex thought she just looked very, very tired.

"I'm taking the bus to the Mission in Calistoga," she said. "I'll be there overnight. So I won't be there when *he* comes to get you."

"*Who*, Mom?" said Joe.

Lisbeth's grey gaze went oddly distant. She put a hand on Joe's shoulder. It was not a natural gesture; her shoulders were stiff and tight, and Joe shrank back a little under her touch. "Tell him it hasn't been so bad here, would you?" she said. "I don't want…well, I don't want him to worry too much."

She took a deep breath, turned, and left. The bell on the door jingled again. Alex stepped out from behind the shelf.

"What was that about?" he asked.

Joe turned to him, his eyes as wide as dinner plates. "You have to take me home," he said. "Right now."

Alex and Joe helped Richard and Katharina bag up the body parts for Maureen, and then they were off, Richard and Katharina back to the cannery, and Alex and Joe towards Nowhere Station and the Feeneys' cheap kit house. Alex pedalled as fast as he dared, Joe clinging to his shoulders as he sped through Nowhere, swerving to avoid patches of ice, and careened onto the the side streets that were the fastest route to the wrong part of town.

The kit house sat on a sad little bluff a short distance back from the lake. It had a handful of just-as-cheap neighbours that had once been painted cheerful colours, but that had quickly faded with the California sun and the wind that whipped across Clear Lake in the cold months and pelted everything with water and pine needles.

Joe's house was the saddest of the lot. It wasn't particularly in disrepair; certainly no more than its neighbours. But where the other kit houses at least had some attempt at homeyness in hand-painted mailboxes or strings of Christmas lights, Joe's house just sat, a tired, greyish blue, nothing more than a box of a house with squat, square windows. It wasn't a home at all: just a place Joe slept, and ate mostly beans, and stared sullenly at the wall while his mother listened to the radio.

Joe was off the bike before Alex even stopped it. Alex had never seen him so eager to get inside the sad little kit house. Normally when Alex biked him home, Joe lingered outside for one last joke or game of roshambeau, before shambling towards the door with his shoulders hunched and his feet dragging. This time Joe sprinted for the door, wrenching it open so violently Alex was afraid it would come right off its cheap hinges.

Alex followed as quickly as he could. Joe was already in the kitchen, tearing through the piles of papers on the yellowing formica. Envelopes and typewritten pages went everywhere, flying through the air and coming to rest all over the coarse carpet.

Joe turned to Alex, clutching an envelope in his hands. "It's him, Alex," he breathed. "It's him!"

He walked into the living room as though he were in a daze, staring at the squat, square envelope. Alex crossed the living room to join him. He had never seen Joe like this before, all focus and no jokes. Joe was holding the envelope as though he was afraid it would burst into flames – or give him the secrets of the universe. It was hard to tell which.

"What is it?" Alex asked, sitting on down on the faded pink couch as Joe did.

Joe showed him the envelope. It was smallish, maybe the size of a card, and of heavy cream paper. The corners were a little puckered, and the seal strained; whatever was inside was folded thicker than the envelope had been designed to contain. On the front, written in a thick, slightly-blotchy pen with no address, were the words "Joseph Feeney".

"It's from my dad," Joe breathed, his blue-grey eyes welling with tears.

Joe's dad had always sent a card for Christmas, Joe said. No matter how many times his mother had taken him away, no matter the fights, no matter where they ended up: he always sent a card. Even after he had gone to war, those first two years, he had sent a card. It wasn't until Lisbeth had dragged them to Nowhere and left no address that the cards had stopped coming, but Joe always knew. Somehow, the cards would come again.

"He always pretended they were from Santa," Joe said, with a breathless giggle. "It was our little joke. He'd make up some excuse for not sending me anything, like a reindeer was sick or there was an accident with the sleigh."

Joe looked at Alex with fire in his eyes. "If he's found out where we are, he must be coming to take me away," he said. "I'm going to see my dad again!"

He drew in a deep, hiccuping breath, clutching the card. Alex felt his heart thudding in his mouth, echoing the beat of Joe's ecstatic hope.

Joe ripped open the envelope.

The papers inside were folded tightly, over and over on themselves until they made up a thickly-wadded packet. Joe unfolded them with trembling hands. Several times he had to stop and take a breath, his hands shaking so badly he almost tore the paper. Alex itched to get in there and help him, but somehow he knew this was something Joe needed to do alone.

The contents of the envelope were finally spread out on the coffee table. Joe and Alex stared at them.

"I don't get it," said Alex. Joe just shook his head.

There was a postcard that Alex recognised as one of the ones Mr Gentry sold in his store. It had a picture of Clear Lake and the words "Welcome to Nowhere" on the front. There was no address or stamp on the back: just a listing of random letters and numbers Alex couldn't decipher.

Then there was a map of Nowhere itself, printed on a gossamer-thin square of silk. The detail was exquisite: Alex could see every single house, store, and street in hair-thin lines of red, brown, and black. Other details too small to interpret dotted the map in pinpricks of colour, and across the top was what Alex assumed to be the key and scale, though they didn't look anything like the maps Alex had studied in school.

There were other papers, too: a list of what looked like sewing supplies; an anatomical diagram of a person, annotated with symbols and near-illegible notes; a handful of newspaper clippings; the lyrics to some Christmas carols; and a crude-but-detailed drawing of some kind of creature with beady eyes, thick fur, and wickedly-curved horns. Alex couldn't make any sense of it.

"Why would he send me this?" Joe asked, staring at the mess of papers on the table.

"*How* would he send you this?" Alex answered, picking up the postcard of Nowhere. "There's only one place you can even get these postcards. How would your dad get hold of one?"

Joe jumped to his feet, excitement flushing his cheeks again. "Maybe he's already here!" he cried. "Maybe it's a game and I'm meant to find him!"

Alex swallowed. He hated the thought of letting Joe down, but it still didn't make sense. A game came with rules; a treasure hunt had clues. Alex couldn't figure out what tied the postcard, the silk map, and the random papers together. He reached for the envelope, still full-looking from having had so much paper crammed inside, to see whether there was something they had missed.

There was a lump still in there, disguised as the messy folds of an overstuffed envelope. Alex tipped the envelope upside-down over his hand, and gave it a shake.

The other ear fell out.

8

Alex pulled Richard, Maureen, and Katharina aside as Joe put the ear and the papers on the table along with the rest of the body parts.

"It's got him too," Alex whispered. "The mind control."

Katharina gasped. "What do you mean?"

Alex stole a furtive look over his shoulder to Joe, who was handling his own disembodied ear as though he got them in the mail every day, even as he was shudderingly careful not to touch the other parts.

"It's really weird," Alex said. "He barely reacted to the ear. I asked him about the other parts on the way over here – whether he was getting used to them or anything. He still thinks everything else is completely gross, but this one ear doesn't bother him at all."

"Have we encountered anyone else who's interacted with multiple parts?" Maureen asked. Alex could see her running through hypotheses in her head.

"Yeah," Richard said. "Us."

He was right. All of the Liars had got body parts in their presents or stockings. All of them had encountered at least a few other parts. So far, Joe was the only one to have such a muted reaction to any of them.

"D'you think," said Richard, "maybe his dad…"

"Careful," Alex warned. He didn't want to go down that road unless they had a very good reason. Not with how strangely Joe was already acting.

"So?" said Katharina. "What do we do?"

"There's some kind of code," Alex said. "On the postcard, and maybe the map. You're good at puzzles, Katharina. Think you can figure it out?"

Katharina set to work on the map and papers, while Maureen showed the boys what she'd managed to figure out from the body parts.

"They're living cells," she said, holding up a wafer-thin sliver of flesh on one of her microscope slides. "Slow, barely moving, but alive. And there's more."

She picked up the left hand that had come from Katharina's mitten and held it up to the light. "See here?" she said, pointing to the base of the thumb. The others peered at it, hesitant to get too close but unsure what they were supposed to be looking at. Maureen sighed in exasperation and thrust the hand right under Alex's nose.

"Look at the thumb!" she said.

Swallowing back bile, Alex looked closely at the hand. There, right at the bottom knuckle of the thumb, was a thin, pale line, drawn right across the base of the thumb. Maureen turned the hand as Alex looked, and he saw that the line circled all the way around, perfectly even and smooth.

"Is that…" Alex said, swallowing. "Is that a scar?"

"*Exactly,*" said Maureen. "This thumb has been cut off and reattached perfectly."

"Is that even possible?" Alex asked, his mind reeling.

Maureen shook her head. "My dad says we're years away from that kind of surgery. And that's not all."

She led the boys back over to the table. The eyeball was still perched on top of its candlestick, and the two feet were set side-by-side next to it. The ears were set in front of the feet, and there was a space in front of the candlestick where the hand had been.

On the other side of the candlestick was the torso, and on top of the torso was the neck.

Maureen had aligned the neck almost exactly. The slight bulge of the throat curved smoothly into the space between the clavicles; the tendons on either side flowed into the muscles of the shoulders. Alex could see the gap in the smooth, peachy flesh between the neck and the torso, but the pieces definitely fit.

"Take a look between the pieces," Maureen said.

"What?" Alex asked.

"Trust me," Maureen said.

Fighting against the violent clenching of his stomach, Alex reached out to the place where the neck met the torso. The soft, waxy flesh gave under his fingers as they slipped into the gap, the open ends of neck and torso unnervingly warm against his living flesh. He reached in a little further…and stopped, his breath catching in his throat.

Maureen nodded slowly, her eyes bright as twin moons behind her thick glasses. "They're *joining*," she said.

The two pieces were not truly separate any more. Alex's fingers had met one of the arteries in the neck, thick and rough as a guitar string, and it was no longer cut. With a shuddering breath, he moved his hand a little to the left and felt the cartilage of the throat, ribbed beneath his probing fingers, continue seamlessly from neck down into torso.

With a slight, sucking *flllp*, Alex pulled his fingers free and turned to Maureen.

"That's not *possible*," he breathed, his voice rough in his throat.

"It shouldn't be," said Maureen, "but it is. The pieces are putting themselves back together. I wish I'd known before I started aligning them; I'd have been more careful. I'd have sewn them in place to be sure -"

"That's it!" Katharina cried, startling everyone.

Maureen and the boys crowded around her; Katharina pulled the list of sewing supplies free of the other papers.

"Thread of a certain kind, needles of a certain thickness, markers to make the right length of stitches…it's for putting the parts back together!

Like a surgeon with the right tools!"

Maureen snatched the paper away and peered at it. From her sudden gasp and the flush of excitement in her cheeks, Alex knew that Katharina was right. They were supposed to stitch the parts back together, and someone was trying to show them how.

"And that's not all," Katharina said. "See these symbols" – she pulled out the anatomical drawing – "here? In the purple and the green?"

She laid the silk map on the table, pulling the section that showed the shore of the lake taut so that the finely-printed details showed clearly against the white of the papers below.

"This here" – she pointed – "is Maureen's house, and it has this symbol in green. Here on the diagram, by the eye: it's the same symbol! And over here…" She shifted the map so that Downtown Nowhere was clearest, with some of the nearest avenues visible as well. "This is Emma Cagliostro's house, with this mark in purple. Over here, on the right ear – do you see it?"

Richard's jaw dropped with all the suddenness of a cartoon. "It's a treasure map!" he gasped. He leaned in, matching up the symbols with impressive speed. "Right foot…here's Alex's house… left foot…there's mine…the symbol for the torso's here on the Red House…"

"What about the code on the postcard?" Alex asked. "Any luck with that?"

"I think it's instructions for assembling the body," Katharina said. "The symbols correspond to the anatomical diagram, and the letters and numbers match the equipment list. See, here?"

Alex couldn't decipher code as well as Katharina, but he was convinced. The tiny, delicate symbols matched those on the diagram and the map, and he could see some common ground between the combinations of characters and the shorthand for the items on the equipment list.

Richard snatched up one of the other papers. "Oh, look at this!" he said. It was a newspaper clipping: a picture from the front, from a few months or a year ago, showing a soldier in uniform pointing his rifle at some unseen foe. On the barrel of the rifle was a neat little symbol, scrawled in green; Richard pulled the anatomical diagram out of Katharina's hands and held it up next to the clipping. The same little green symbol that marked the rifle in the photograph was on the torso of the diagram – and the exact same symbol was drawn on the Red House on the silk map of Nowhere.

"No way," Alex breathed. "It's telling us where the parts are, and what presents they're in."

The plan came together quickly after that. Katharina efficiently matched the symbols between the newspaper clippings, the anatomical diagram, and the map, and soon they had a good idea of where every remaining part was and what was likely to disguise it. If they split up and spread out, they could have them all together by mid-afternoon.

Alex noticed that Katharina gave particular attention to the silk map, and not just to match the symbols to those on the scattered papers. There was something faraway in her eyes as she traced the lines printed on the tissue-thin fabric, following the streets through Nowhere as they spilled onto the road that circumnavigated Clear Lake. He thought he knew what she was thinking, but he bit back his questions. He would ask her later, when the Liars weren't all together.

"I still don't understand one thing," said Richard, as they all confirmed their missions and took their newspaper clippings to remind them what to look for. "What's this all for? Why send mind-controlling body parts all around Nowhere – and why send us to go collect them?"

"It's a mission," Joe said firmly. "A secret mission from my dad."

He looked around the group, his eyes alight with conviction. "The war isn't over when it's over, right?" he said. "You don't just pop off some firecrackers and come home. There's cleanup, and hunting down spies, and other…stuff. My dad wants us to help with a secret mission, and when it's done he can come home and take me away. And we'll all be heroes, won't we?"

"Sure," said Alex. "That must be it."

9

The hunt for the remaining body parts went much more quickly with the map. They spread out on their bikes, Joe riding tandem with whoever would let him, and set off for the houses marked with the spidery little symbols on the silk.

Eugene Brady had an arm tucked into the sleeve of a new sweater.

Sissy Lohengrin had a leg stuffed into a toy farmhouse, crowding out all the little wooden cows.

Callum Carnegie didn't realise he had the other eyeball in his bag of candied cherries until he bit into it, and Katharina had to go chasing after it when it dropped out of his hand and rolled into the bushes while he bent over and threw up everything he'd eaten for a week. Katharina was in an incandescent rage as she packed snow into the front of her boots in an attempt to wash out the chunks of regurgitated cherries, and insisted on having a partner for the rest of her hunt.

They changed groups often, handing off body

parts so one or another of them could run them back to the attic of the cannery, and trading bikeless Joe from one partner to the next. They didn't particularly plan who was going where or with whom; it just happened naturally that the pairings shifted as they spread out around town, then coalesced back together again to compare notes.

Alex certainly did not plan to be partnered with Maureen, standing at Tommy Waid's front door, looking for a butt.

At sixteen, Tommy Waid was the oldest of the kids that the map said would have a part. It didn't seem weird, though, because Tommy was much more like a kid the Liars' age than their teenage siblings. He'd been held back in school a couple times and was still a slow reader, and he much preferred playing games of tag and catch out in the woods than driving into town to buy magazines or talk about girls. Despite his size and the thin fuzz on his upper lip, Tommy didn't seem all that interested in growing up. That suited the kids who liked him just fine.

Alex felt a brief sting of guilt as Tommy's mom, Ellen, called out to her son that he had friends over. The truth was, Alex liked Tommy a lot, but he didn't really think of him as a friend. He was fun to play with in a cheerful, teddy-bear kind of way, but Alex didn't spare much thought for him when he wasn't hanging out with them in a big group – or unwittingly holding on to something Alex and the other Liars needed to solve a mystery. As Tommy came around the corner, his wide-set eyes almost disappearing in the cheerful smile that took up most of his broad face, Alex decided he could spare a few minutes to actually spend time with Tommy while Maureen tried to find the present.

To Alex's surprise, Tommy had something new to talk about. Usually he was all about toys and comic books, or the latest developments in his favourite radio dramas, but this time Tommy had an announcement.

"I'm going to work on a farm!" he said, as delighted as though he were announcing an invitation to Santa Claus' workshop.

"For real?" Alex asked. He found it hard to imagine Tommy with a job, Tommy getting a paycheck…Tommy growing up.

Tommy nodded enthusiastically, his smile showing all his teeth. "I'm starting after Christmas," he said. "It's a pear farm. I'm going to help with planting, and with picking, and with keeping the trees healthy…"

"Just odd jobs to start with," Ellen said, emerging from the kitchen with mugs of hot chocolate. "It's the Hansons' orchard, up the hill. They've always had a soft spot for Tommy."

Alex took a sip of hot chocolate to hide that he wasn't quite sure what to say. He knew the Hansons – their twins were a few years older than him and about to leave school – and they were good people. Tommy working among the pear trees, spending time outdoors, keeping company with the twins, wasn't a bad mental image at all. He wasn't sure why he felt so complicated about it.

"He can't stay in school forever," Ellen said, as though she had read his mind. "And he gets lonely with nothing but his comics and the radio. You know, I'm glad you came over today," she said. "He's been dying to tell people."

Out of the corner of his eye, Alex saw Maureen squirm uneasily as she scanned the presents under the tree for something the right size or shape. She wasn't as comfortable around Tommy as the rest of the Liars: her blunt, often cheerless directness didn't mesh well with Tommy's open enthusiasm for just about everything.

"We're actually…" Alex started to say, then he interrupted his own sentence with another sip of hot chocolate. He was aware that Maureen was staring intently at him, willing him to get on with it so they could find the present and get moving. He was just as aware that Tommy was waiting patiently to tell him more about the pear orchard and share his excitement with someone who wasn't his mother. After the day Alex had already had – the foot, the ear, the mad dash around town to find other bits of an unknown kid who was probably dead but improbably knitting himself back together – Alex really liked the idea of sitting with the hot chocolate and listening to Tommy tell him everything there was to know about farming pears.

He sighed into his mug. "Can Tommy come out and play with me tomorrow?" he asked. "Only we're actually here on business today, and I'm afraid we can't stay very long."

Tommy's smile faded. "You aren't here to visit me?" he asked.

Alex gulped, suddenly realising how cruel it would be to tell Tommy not only that he wasn't really here to hang out, but also that he needed to take one of his presents. He looked at Maureen for help.

"We need to take one of these," Maureen said bluntly, crouching to get a better look at the presents.

"Oh, my!" said Ellen, as Tommy's smile faded even more. "Whatever for?"

"This wrapping paper is from Gentry's General Store, isn't it?" Maureen pointed to the cheery red-and-gold striped paper that covered most of the packages under the tree. Ellen nodded.

"There was an accident at the paper factory and some toxic chemicals got mixed into the print dye," Maureen lied smoothly. "My father's testing one present per household to make sure the rest are safe to open tomorrow."

"My goodness," said Ellen. "That's very kind of him, to work on Christmas Eve. Can you take any present, or must it be something specific?"

"Anything will do," Maureen said, "as long as it's about the size of a human pelvis."

Ellen blinked, and Tommy giggled. "You're looking for a butt!" he cried.

Maureen nodded solemnly. "Yes," she said. "We're hoping to find a butt."

Ellen put down her hot chocolate and looked over at the presents under the tree. "I believe," she said, with a sidelong look at her son, "that Tommy asked Santa for some new swim briefs this Christmas. Would that be about right?"

That sounded promising to both Maureen and Alex – the newspaper clipping that matched the symbol for Tommy's house on the map had an article about a swimming pool – so Ellen pointed out the right package for them, a lumpy, square-ish bundle about as wide across as Alex's hips. Alex handed the present to Tommy to open; it seemed like the right thing to do.

The swim briefs were a few sizes too big for the pelvis inside them, and they sagged inelegantly. Tommy's eyes widened at the sight.

"It really is a butt!" he cried. His face fell. "Mom," he said, "did I get sent someone else's bathing suit?"

"Of course not, dear," Ellen said. "Why would you think that?"

Tommy shrugged. "Because it has someone else's butt in it."

Even Maureen let out an amused snort at that.

"We should give it back," Tommy said firmly. "It's not fair to take someone else's bathing suit."

Alex couldn't resist. "Or someone else's butt?" he asked.

Tommy nodded seriously. Maureen laughed out loud, and Ellen shot her a disapproving look.

Maureen bit her lip.

Alex thought quickly. "It's just a little mix-up, Tommy," he said. "The briefs are alright, they just got sent with an extra butt. If you let me keep the butt, I can take it back to its rightful owner and everything'll be fine. Okay?"

Tommy's broad brow furrowed in a thoughtful frown. Alex didn't blame him for finding the idea of a disembodied pelvis a bit much to handle. Even for someone as good at taking things in stride as Tommy, this was pretty weird. Finally he nodded, and handed the too-big briefs and the pelvis over to Alex. "I hope you find who it belongs to," he said seriously. "I wouldn't like to be missing my butt."

"Me neither," Alex said with absolute sincerity. He went to pull the pelvis out of the swim briefs, then paused. He did not relish the idea of cycling around Nowhere with a pair of naked buttocks in the basket of his bicycle.

Ellen smiled wryly at his hesitation. "I'll lend you some underwear," she said.

"I'm not like him, you know," Maureen said as she and Alex pedalled back towards downtown.

Alex looked over at her in surprise. "So what if you are?" he asked. "Tommy's cool."

"He's different," Maureen said.

Alex felt a swell of indignation that, if he'd stopped to think about it, he would have realised was mostly guilt. "So?" he asked hotly. "So are you!"

"I know," Maureen said. "That's the point. Not all different people are the same."

Alex shook his head angrily. "What's that supposed to mean?"

Maureen was quiet for a moment, except for the sound of her pedalling.

"I know I'm not good at certain things," she said at last. "Like making friends, or cracking jokes, or being happy all the time."

"So?" said Alex. "None of that matters to me."

"That's because you're my friend," said Maureen. "It matters to other people."

"Does it matter to you?"

Maureen thought about that for a little while. "Not mostly," she said finally.   "I like you and Richard and Joe and Katharina, and I like science and math and patterns. Most of the time that's fine.

"But sometimes it isn't, you know?   I'll say something that seems perfectly sensible, and then everyone's giving me weird looks or laughing at me. Even the teachers do it. Like I'll answer a question correctly, but it's not the kind of correctly they're expecting, and then somehow it's a problem even though I'm right, and all I'm trying for is to be right. And I never know what I've done wrong to make people look at me like that.

"So then people get all quiet, or they talk to me like I'm stupid, or put me in special classes, and I realise: they're treating me just like Tommy, even though we're different *kinds* of different.   And I want to tell them it's not fair to do that, because he can do all the things that I can't."

"Like what?"

"Like get people to like him.   Like have fun in the snow without trying to figure out exactly how cold it is and what that means for the friction coefficient of our shoes.   Like get excited about working on a pear farm."

She stopped talking, and Alex knew that in her characteristic Maureen way, she had run out of things to say on the matter and wasn't going to try to fill the silence.   He also knew she was still thinking about it, because he knew she never stopped thinking about things.

"Maureen," Alex said sincerely, "you're the smartest person I know.   You can do *anything*. You're going to go to college and be a scientist and discover new planets or the cure for cancer or something. Tommy's going to work on a pear farm for the rest of his life."

"And he's going to be really happy the whole time," Maureen said. "I wish I could learn how to do that."

10

They were almost done. While Maureen and Alex had been negotiating for the pelvis, Katharina and Joe had gathered up their parts and headed back to the cannery to meet them. Richard arrived a few minutes later with a bag full of sewing supplies he'd raided from his mom's things. Maureen set immediately to assembling the parts, while Joe, still convinced that there was a secret message from his dad in the mess of newspaper clippings and carol lyrics, helped Richard sort the sewing supplies according to the symbols on the postcard.

That left Alex and Katharina, both feeling a little queasy at the sight of Maureen confidently sewing the gap between the neck and torso closed with a neat, white whip stitch.

"I didn't think Maureen was so domestic," Katharina whispered to Alex.

"She isn't," Alex whispered back. "She taught herself taxidermy."

They didn't have to agree on anything; they just

backed slowly out of the cannery and left the others to their gruesome work.

There were two parts left. They found the first easily: Freddie Maas, who had aspirations to baseball stardom, had asked for a new catcher's mitt for Christmas, and had found a right hand in it. It didn't take much persuading for Katharina to get him to hand it over; she just had to agree to help him re-wrap the mitt so his parents wouldn't know he had opened it. Alex offered to help too, but Freddie mumbled something about it being neater with just two people and then insisted that Alex sit all the way over on the other side of the living room while he and Katharina worked on the present over by the tree. When they were done, Freddie wrapped the hand in a scarf and presented it to Katharina as though it were some kind of magnificent gift. He asked her, with wide eyes and a squeak in his voice, if she'd come back and tell him what happened when she was done with the mystery.

He seemed to have forgotten Alex was there at all.

"I think he likes you," Alex said, once they were outside and back on their bikes.

"Oh God, I hope not," Katharina said, unwrapping the hand and using the scarf as extra protection against the icy wind that had suddenly kicked up. "I just heard more about baseball in the last ten minutes than I wanted to in my entire life."

Alex grinned. Even with Richard all googly-eyed over Emma Cagliostro, they weren't going to lose a Liar to a stupid crush today.

They had deliberately left the head until last. It wasn't exactly by spoken agreement; they were all just uncomfortably aware that, no matter how creepy it was having a pair of eyeballs – one slightly chewed – staring at them from the table in the cannery attic, having an actual head looking their way would be infinitely worse.

Alex and Katharina stopped at a cafe just off Main Street, where wide parasols over outdoor tables gave them a relatively sheltered flat surface to take another look at the map. Alex spread the translucent silk delicately over the wooden tabletop, careful not to let it catch on splinters. They put their heads together and squinted at the map, finding the last symbol at the end of a cul-de-sac not too far from Alex's house.

Alex noticed Katharina's eyes wandering up to the key and scale at the top of the map. The key made no sense at all – it didn't seem to indicate rivers or roads or types of buildings, but was just a series of symbols: red wine glass, green maze, blue train, orange barrel. The scale was a little more familiar, but Alex didn't recognise the units of measurement; they looked more like runes than numbers.

He glanced at Katharina. "Are you thinking what I'm thinking?" he asked.

Katharina kept her eyes on the map. "What are you thinking?" she asked back.

Alex swallowed. This was delicate territory with Katherina. But she was the only other person who might see the map the same way he did. "My dad," he said hesitantly, "had a map like this sewn into his jacket when he was shipped out. In case he was captured and needed to find his way back."

"My parents were smuggled one when they defected," Katharina said. "It was cut up into fifty-two pieces and hidden in a deck of cards." She tore her eyes away from the key and looked at Alex. "You're partly right," she said. "This *is* an escape map. My mother even helped print them for a while, as a show of good faith after my parents came over."

"My mom sewed my dad's into a scarf."

"But who would make an escape map of Nowhere?" Katharina asked, turning her attention back to the map. "If an American soldier is captured and makes it all the way to Nowhere, they're already home safe. Silk maps are for enemy territory, not little towns in California."

"What about" — Alex hesitated even to say it — "captured German soldiers?"

Katharina laughed, and Alex breathed a sigh of relief. "My parents said this was never really a German thing. British, mostly, and they shared it with the Americans."

"So…"

"I don't know. It could be from Joe's father, just as he insists. It could be there's some secret German operation here I just don't know about."

"Is there?"

"My parents are seismologists and I don't know what you're talking about," Katharina said coolly. She looked back up at Alex. "I think it's clear this map and the body parts belong to the same operation. I think it might be that Joe's father is involved. But I know one thing for certain."

"What's that?" asked Alex.

"That we won't know anything for certain until we get that head."

They arrived at the cul-de-sac to find nine-year-old Kyle Brenner sitting on the front porch, chin set sullenly on his knees and his eyes red from crying. He gave them a surly look as they approached.

"My brother isn't here, so you can go away," he said.

Alex frowned. "Why would we want to talk to your brother?" he asked. Beside him, Katharina shuddered.

Kyle shrugged his tightly-hunched shoulders. "I dunno, because you're friends at school or something?"

"Just because we're in the same class," Alex said, "does *not* mean we're friends."

Katharina nodded in vigorous agreement. Julian Brenner and his cohort were the school's biggest bullies. Julian had always been cruel, but when his growth spurt hit early and he shot up to tower over even Richard, he had become unspeakable. Sure, there were mean older kids who had more size and weight than him, but even the worst of them was better than Julian, simply because they were in different classes and preferred to drive into Santa Mira on the weekends than to hang around Nowhere and mess with other kids. The older kids were bullies of opportunity, picking on whoever was nearby because it was easy. Julian treated bullying like a career choice: he *worked* at it, and his favourite targets – the ones for whom he reserved the very best of his cruelty – were the members of the Liars' Club. Richard was the only one with a chance against Julian and his boys in a fight; Alex was lucky that Julian had never quite found a cruelty particular enough to stick to him. And that was good, because Joe, Maureen, and Katharina had suffered enough beatings and shredded self-esteem for even Richard's and Alex's fair share.

Alex sat on the porch next to Kyle. He liked the younger kid, even if he usually steered clear of him just to avoid attracting Julian's attention. Kyle was sweet, and imaginative, and a bit shy, and now he was crying as though someone had cancelled Christmas.

"Hey," Alex said. "Whatever's happening, I bet you're having a better day than I am."

Even through his tears, Kyle's expression was absolutely withering. "Am not," he sniffed. "Julian made me open all my presents so he could take them and I'd get in trouble. And I think he messed with one of them just to scare me."

Alex caught Katharina's eye. "What do you mean?" he asked.

Kyle's tears, slowed while he had been talking, started flowing freely again. "I wanted a cowboy hat," he said, using sobs for punctuation. "I wanted it…all year…it's the only thing I asked for in my letter to Santa…"

"And?" Alex prodded gently.

"And it had a stupid horrible fake head in it!" Kyle bawled.

"Are you sure it was fake?" Katharina asked. Once again, Alex was impressed by how much disdain the nine-year-old could pack into a single withering look, especially when he was still busy crying.

"No," Kyle said, "Julian really went out and *killed* someone just so he could cut off their head and put it in my Christmas present."

"It's not so big a stretch," Katharina muttered. Alex elbowed her in the shin.

"So what happened to it?" Alex asked.

"Julian took it!" Kyle wailed.

"The head?"

"And…and…and the *haaaaaat!*" The word disappeared into a drawn-out wail of despair. Alex patted Kyle on the shoulder with what he hoped was reassurance, but he was distracted. Having to get the head back from Julian was not something the Liars had planned for, but it was the last piece of the puzzle, and Alex was somehow sure that putting the rest of the body together wouldn't mean a thing without a head to put on top.

Katharina must have figured out what he was thinking, because she nudged him hard with her foot and hissed, "Don't you dare!"

Alex ignored her. He took a deep breath. "Kyle," he said. "Where did Julian go?"

"T-to the meadow, I th-think," Kyle sniffed.

Alex sighed deeply as he stood. "Kyle," he said, "we're going to get your hat back."

11

The "meadow" was really just a patch of land behind some houses that wasn't big enough for a ranch, but that hadn't been developed into more houses yet. It had short, scratchy grass and a handful of stubby apple trees. Right in the middle, where a shallow ditch with some standing water had aspirations as a pond, Julian Brenner and two of his brawniest friends were kicking a human head back and forth between them like a soccer ball.

Alex had no idea what his plan was as he laid down his bike at the end of the meadow and started walking out into the snow-dusted grass. Half of him hoped they'd get bored with what they were doing and leave the head behind before he reached them. Katharina stayed back with the bikes, not out of sight – there wasn't much cover available without going all the way back to the street – but ready to turn tail and bolt if she had to. Julian and his friends could be especially cruel to Katharina.

The boys kept kicking the head around. As Alex got closer, he could see that it had a mop of dark, curly hair, and a spray of freckles across an upturned nose. The eyelids flapped loosely over their empty sockets, and between that and the overall movement of the head as it was kicked from one twelve-year-old brute to another, it was hard to tell how old the head was. Nonetheless, Alex got an impression, just as he had from the feet, of someone pretty close to his age.

Somehow, that made the fact that Julian and his goons were using it as a football a lot worse.

They showed no sign of losing interest in the head, so Alex squared his shoulders, took a deep breath, and yelled the most forceful thing he could think of, which turned out to be "H-hey?"

Julian stopped mid-kick, and the head plopped off his foot and made a sad little bounce into the snowy grass. Alex swallowed. He was off to a bad start.

"Can I have that?" he asked, pointing to the head.

It was probably the stupidest thing he could have asked. Maureen would have come up with some scary story about the head being radioactive; Richard would have pretended to be willing to fight for it and probably gotten away with it. Joe would have said something even more stupid and distracted Julian and his boys by getting beaten up – it would have hurt, but it would have worked.

Anything was better than just asking Julian for something, because when you asked Julian for something, he found the cruelest way possible to stop you getting it.

Julian picked up the head and held it by the hair. The mouth sagged limply open. "You want this?" Julian asked, his friends snickering behind him.

Alex decided he might as well go all in. "And the hat," he said, pointing to the goon who was wearing it, comically undersized on his big, flat head. "Kyle's pretty upset you took it."

Julian's friend didn't need to be told how to react. He took the cowboy hat off his head and flung it into the ditch, where the muddy water started leaching into the suede at once. For good measure, the goon jumped on it, printing a muddy bootprint into the crown and splashing mud all up the legs of his pants. Alex let out an involuntary sigh: it was all so predictable.

Almost immediately, he realised that the sigh was just as stupid as the question. Suddenly Julian was holding the head right up to his face, nose to waxy, freckled nose, and Alex's field of vision was full of those awful, slack eyelids.

"You want *this*?" Julian repeated, his own snarling face right next to the head's.

"Yes…please?" Alex swallowed. He could all but hear Katharina rolling her eyes from the edge of the meadow. He really should have had a better plan.

Julian sneered. "Don't you want to know how I got this?" he asked.

"Not really," Alex said. Julian ignored him.

"Caught some stupid drifter kid out by the caves," Julian said. "Thought he could pull a knife on me and steal my stuff. So I took that knife off of him, and I broke both his hands, and then I cut off his head. Do you know what it's like to watch the life go out of someone's eyes, you stupid kid?"

Alex couldn't help himself: he burst out laughing. For a second, Julian looked totally dumbfounded. Alex could sort of understand it; on any ordinary day, he would absolutely have believed that Julian had beheaded some hapless kid, and he would have been wetting himself with fear. Unfortunately for both of them, it was not an ordinary day.

Julian's fist in his solar plexus brought his laughter to an abrupt halt. Suddenly blows were raining down, bone-bruising punctuations to Julian's red-faced, spittle-flecked rage. "Don't... you...DARE...laugh...at...me!" Julian screamed, a vicious punch between every word. Alex dropped to the grass and curled up, trying to protect his stomach with his knees and elbows. The head thumped to the ground beside him as Julian dropped it to use both fists, but Alex couldn't even reach out to grab it and run under the relentless hail of blows.

Suddenly he heard a shriek from across the meadow, and he looked up just in time to see Julian stagger back as a disembodied hand struck him savagely across the face. The hand bounced off his cheek and fell into the grass, but right behind it was Katharina, screaming furiously in German and driving her elbow right into Julian's ribs. For one, glorious moment, she looked to Alex like an avenging Valkyrie, brown hair flying loose out of its braids, fists flying as fast and hard as her frenzied German cursing.

It didn't last. Julian was much bigger than Katharina, and he had two equally-bulky friends. One of them grabbed Katharina by the hair; the other wrenched her arm back, and all at once she was small, shy Katharina again, looking pathetically fragile against the massive meat of Julian's two goons. Alex tried to scramble to his feet, but Julian planted a foot on his shoulder and flattened him back down. As Julian turned his attention to Katharina, Alex managed to grab the head and drag it towards him, hiding it against his stomach in his protective curl.

Julian leered at Katharina. "Nice try, Kraut," he spat. "In case you hadn't heard, you lost the war. Or can't you read American newspapers, Winter-*kraut*?"

"Wintertraub," Katharina snarled. "My name is Katharina Winter*traub*."

"*Kraut*erina."

"*Schweinehund!*"

Katherina shrieked as Julian grabbed her arm and twisted it viciously.

"Stop that!" Alex yelled.

Julian cackled. "What's the matter, pip-squeak? Scared for your Nazi girlfriend?"

"She's not…a Nazi…" Alex said through gritted teeth. He managed to get to his knees, but didn't see how to get upright without revealing the head – and inviting another beating from Julian.

"Looks like a Nazi," Julian said cruelly. "Talks

like a Nazi. Got two Nazi parents."

"My parents are *scientists*," Katharina said. Alex wished she would just shut up, but this was Julian's horrible gift. He always knew just what to poke at to get you to fight back, and then when he beat you to a pulp it somehow made sense in his sick, meaty head.

"How about it, guys?" Julian asked, aiming his wicked sneer at his friends. "I think the world would be better with one less Nazi Kraut in it." Suddenly there was a pocket knife in his hand – Alex hadn't even seen him pull it out – and Alex's heart sprang into his mouth. Katherina went deathly silent.

"So I didn't cut that other head off," Julian said, only just loud enough for Alex to hear. "Doesn't mean I can't take yours."

"Jules," one of the goons said, looking suddenly worried. "There are houses, like, *right there*."

"So?" Julian asked, still terrifyingly quiet. "Who'd care about seeing a little Nazi get what she deserves? They'd probably think I'm a hero."

The goon shifted his weight uneasily. "Yeah, but...but *Jules*..."

For a heart-stopping second Julian just stared at Katharina, pocket knife in his hand, a sadistic shine in his eyes. Then in one swift movement he crouched, picked up the hand, and swiped Katharina across the face with it as he stood. Alex saw tears spring to her eyes, but she held his gaze bitterly.

"Come on," Julian spat, and the two goons let go

of Katharina. Her legs went out beneath her and she dropped to the grass, breathing heavily. Julian tossed the hand to one of his goons, and turned away to the trees at the far end of the meadow.

"*Verrückter*," Katharina hissed.

Julian turned, raised his big booted foot, and brought it crashing down on Katharina's wrist.

Alex's house was closer than Katharina's, and there was no way Katharina was getting on a bike. Her wrist was already turning an ugly purple where Julian had stamped on it, and she whimpered in pain with every step. Alex tucked the head awkwardly under one arm, and supported Katharina with the other. There was no point worrying about the hand now.

Alex's dad took one look at Katharina's wrist, and snapped to attention. The strange, distant haze that had clouded his green eyes since he had come home disappeared in an instant, and he was up, out of his chair, the flannel blanket dropping to the floor. Though he was only upright for a few steps before he crouched by Katharina to look at her arm, his full height seemed taller than Alex remembered – taller than he'd seen him in months. Alex's mom ran to get his bag, and Alex himself watched, dazed, as his dad took Katharina's hand in his own and gently, gently and efficiently, looked at her purpling wrist to see what the damage was.

"It's okay," he said quietly, soft as if he were soothing a startled cat. "It's okay, I'm just going to take a look. Nothing to be afraid of."

Katharina's hiccupping sobs slowed a little as she let Alex's dad run his fingers over her wrist, feeling softly for anything out of place.

"Does it hurt when I touch here?" he asked.

Katharina nodded.

"How bad?"

"Pretty bad," Katharina said, sniffing.

"We're going to move your hand, okay? You tell me if the pain gets worse."

Alex stayed quiet as he watched his dad gently flex each of Katharina's fingers, then her hand. He was absolutely intent, probing softly, listening to sounds her wrist made as it moved, as focused as Maureen with her microscope. As he worked, he talked, explaining what he was going to do, making little jokes, reassuring Katharina when a movement made her wince in pain.

Alex's mom came to stand by him, holding the medical bag. She sighed heavily. "I hate that your friend got hurt," she said quietly, "but…"

But it's nice to have your dad back. Alex swallowed back a surge of guilt as he silently finished his mom's sentence.

"I don't think it's broken," Alex's dad was saying. "But this is a pretty bad sprain. Let's get it supported for now, and you should see a doctor as soon as possible, okay?"

Katharina nodded, and Alex's dad supported her wrist in his right hand while he rummaged in his bag with his left. He gave a low chuckle, his reassuring gaze never leaving Katharina.

"Alex," he said, "would you bring me my tie from the chair over there? I'm all out of bandages."

Alex sprang to attention. The tie draped over the back of the armchair was an old one, striped blue and a little worn. Alex's dad had had it since before he had left for war.

"I'm going to need your help with this, son," Alex's dad said, as he took the tie between his thumb and forefinger. "This is a ten-finger job."

It was the first time Alex had seen his dad's hand up close, at least since the bandages had come off. The scar down the side was raised and uneven, not smooth and fine like the scar on the disembodied hand. Along the top, where three fingers had once been, the skin was drawn into a puckered seam. There was no scabbing or redness, no angry wound to remember the explosion by. Just those rough, raised lines, and the space where the fingers used to be.

Alex found it easy enough not to look once he got the hang of winding the tie around Katharina's bruised wrist. His dad guided him: tight, but not too tight, layered up around the joint to give it extra support. As Alex tucked the end of the tie snugly into the makeshift bandage, his dad took Katharina's fingers again, slowly flexing them and testing their movement. "Too tight?" he asked. "Any tingling?"

Katharina shook her head. Her face was a mess, her nose red and running and her eyes puffy, but she was no longer crying. She made a slow fist, and took a deep breath.

Alex's dad looked sidelong at him with a smile. "Very nice work," he said.

As Alex's mom came over to retrieve the bag, her foot nudged the head that Alex had dropped on the way in. It rolled over a couple of times, and came to rest by Alex's dad's bag.

Alex's dad looked down at it. Lying face-up, the eyelids sagged over the empty sockets, and the lips pulled back just slightly from the even white teeth into a limp hint of a smile. Alex shuddered and looked at his dad, but his dad just stared at the head, that strange, distant look coming back into his eyes.

"I thought," he said, frowning as he looked at the head, "that Santa brought you a foot for Christmas."

12

The mood in the cannery attic was grim as Alex helped Katharina in through the window and produced the head. He told the others what had happened with Julian, and that the hand was probably gone for good. Richard was ready to ride right out and track Julian down, but Alex persuaded him not to. While it was true that Richard had the best shot at giving Julian a taste of his own medicine, Alex couldn't shake the evil glint in Julian's eyes as he had threatened Katharina with the pocketknife. If the goons hadn't got scared at the last minute, Alex thoroughly believed Katharina might not have made it out alive, and that meant he'd crossed a line that Richard never would.

"Let's just work with what we've got," Maureen said, taking the head and setting it on top of the neck. Joe helped hold it in place while Maureen went to work with the needle, making quick work of the whip-stitch she was now very practiced at using.

Put all together, Alex could see now that his impression had been right. The boy they had assembled from all the parts was twelve, thirteen at most. He was skinny, but not underfed: he had the same sort of wiry thinness as Joe, with sharp elbows and shoulders. Richard had brought some of his clothes to dress the boy, but he was closer to Alex's size than Richard's, and the pants and singlet sagged at the too-big seams. On a sudden impulse, Alex shrugged off his own sweater and shirt, and took the ones that Richard had laid out for the boy. It seemed only fair that the boy have a couple of things that actually fit, instead of swimming in Richard's clothes when he woke up.

Assuming, of course, that he woke up. There was a strange energy to the body that got stronger as Maureen worked. It didn't feel like life, exactly: it wasn't the expectant warmth of a sleeping cat or the quiet vitality of a hibernating squirrel. It was something else – a sense of waiting, of standing by, like the last glow of a candle wick waiting for the gentle breath that would coax it back to full flame.

Maureen pulled back the eyelids, and pushed the eyeballs into place. The left one – the one that Callum Carnegie had started to take a bite out of – took some effort, and Alex worried that Maureen would pop it with the pressure she was applying to get it into its socket. But finally, with a prod and a wet sucking sound, the eyeball popped into place, and Maureen pulled the eyelids closed again, now round and full instead of loose and drooping.

She stepped back to admire her handiwork. The

boy sat propped on the table, chin to his chest, his arms held loosely by his sides. One wrist ended in nothing; on the other, Alex could already see a thin white scar forming where Maureen's neat stitches held the hand in place. The tension in the room rose as all the Liars stared at the boy, waiting for something to happen.

"Did we just stitch together a dead kid?" asked Joe. "Because that feels like a really disgusting waste of time."

"A dead body wouldn't heal itself," Maureen pointed out.

"So what are we waiting on?" asked Richard.

"I don't know," said Maureen.

They argued back and forth for a while. Katharina wondered aloud if they needed all the parts; Alex reassured her that couldn't be it, because he knew she felt guilty about losing the hand. Maureen proposed they just wait for all the seams to knit themselves closed, but Joe was convinced there was some magic ingredient they were missing: an on-switch or a tincture or the machine from that Frankenstein movie.

"The carols," said Richard, out of nowhere. "They're the only thing from the packet we haven't used yet."

"You think they're a code?" Katharina asked. "A set of instructions, for what to do now?"

"I think," Richard said slowly, a little pink with embarrassment, "we maybe have to sing them."

It honestly wasn't any stranger than pieces of a body joining themselves back together after mind-controlling half the town, Alex thought, as Richard and Katharina sorted through the carol lyrics to see if they needed to be in any particular order. Even Maureen was surprisingly easy to get on board; she complained she couldn't sing, but mumbled something about manipulating sonic frequencies and agreed to give it a try anyway.

So they joined hands – because it seemed like the right thing to do – and they sang. Richard and Alex ended up on opposite sides of the boy, Richard holding the reattached hand, and Alex awkwardly circling the stump of a wrist with his fingers. It was a struggle to concentrate on Christmas carols while trying to hold a hand that didn't exist, but luckily the songs were all old ones, the kinds of traditional carols that all the Liars had been singing for as long as they could remember and that felt like they'd been born knowing them. Two of them were even in Latin.

Richard and Katharina had strung them together in an order they thought made some kind of sense, and, with his strong voice that hadn't broken yet but was clearly getting ready to, Richard led the singing. They weren't exactly a prizewinning choir, but all of them felt it: as the carol music swelled, that same strange energy they had felt from the body surged, prickling along their arms and between their joined hands, pulling them together, in tune and in sync. The sounds of Nowhere from outside the cannery window faded; the rustling leaves and twittering birdsong sounded as though they were coming from far, far away, and the sounds of their voices swelled and echoed in ways that seemed impossible in the dusty, low-ceilinged attic.

At some point – and Alex couldn't have pointed out when – they stopped looking at the lyrics, stopped even looking to Richard to lead them. Alex realised he couldn't have stopped singing if he wanted to: the energy that bound them was pulling the words out of him, sucking them into the space in the centre of their circle of joined hands. For a moment, Alex thought he could *see* their singing, not as light or dust or anything solid, but as a sense of otherness superimposed upon reality, pulsing invisibly between them. As they sang the last note of the last carol, the otherness hung in the air, quivering, almost-shimmering, a thrumming *something* heavier than air but too light to touch or define.

Then the body sucked in a great, shuddering breath; the otherness poured into its lungs, and the eyelids snapped open on wide, frightened brown eyes.

"Oh my God," said the boy, looking around at the terrified Liars. "I can't believe it worked."

And then he burst into tears.

He was fine, he said, as the Liars made an awkward show of trying to comfort him as he cried. Just relieved, and tired, and surprised to be alive again. It was a lot to experience at once; no one questioned that. After a while, he started to calm down, and even gratefully accepted Alex's shirt and sweater, but when he tried to put his right arm through the sleeve and realised there was no hand on the end of it, he burst into tears all over again.

With no clue what else to do, Richard started telling the boy about all they had gone through to put him back together. Joe joined in, turning it into a pantomime, and even Katharina, careful of her injured wrist, got in on the action. Whether it was the story itself, the amateur dramatics, or just having something going on that wasn't his own shock, the boy eventually calmed down again, and by the time the Liars were done, he seemed to be ready to talk.

His name was Carl, he said, though he had to think about it for a moment when they asked. As to where he was from, he begged the Liars to believe him, insisted he wasn't as crazy as he was about to sound, and then told them he was an elf, on the run from Santa's workshop.

To his surprise, Alex had no trouble believing it at all. Sometime between the Red House and the carols, he had let go of Maureen's mind control theory and accepted that the truth was much stranger. And, with his tightly-curled hair, pointed ears, and dense splattering of freckles across his button nose, it really was not that hard to imagine that Carl in a pointed hat and curled-toe shoes, working away at toys for Santa.

"So why'd you run away?" Joe asked. "And why come here? Here's Nowhere – literally."

"Because…because it's close to home, I think. Or somewhere home used to be. And because maybe there's something about this place…"

"Hold up," Joe interrupted. "Whaddya mean, 'home'? Elves come from California? What, do they grow 'em on trees?"

"No," Carl said solemnly, though a slight twitch to his lips said he thought the idea was pretty funny. "*I* come from here. I wasn't always an elf. None of us were. Elves are kids. Right up until we become something else."

13

"I ran away from home. I don't remember why. I think back, and it's so faraway and fuzzy, but I don't remember starving or hurting or having much to be afraid of. I remember a place called Calistoga, and I remember wanting to see the world. But family, friends, why I ran away and why I picked then…it's a fog, a snowstorm in my head.

"I came on a train, I remember that much. An old-fashioned train, with a big locomotive. It went for what seemed like forever, and it took me to the workshop, out in the middle of nowhere. Not nowhere like here is Nowhere: *real* nowhere, off the map and out in the stars. A little town dropped in the snow for no reason but to make toys for Christmas, with no one there except the elves and the kids who are going to be elves but don't know it yet.

"There are only three grownups there. There's the stout man, Father Christmas. Santa, Saint Nicholas, whatever you call him. He was always just "the stout man" to me – I think someone…someone I knew…

"There's the Belsnickel. Mr Snickel, we called him. He's the factory foreman. He works you hard, but he ain't mean. He keeps an eye on your work and hits you with a bundle of branches if you do something stupid. It's pretty hard to do anything too stupid, though. Especially after you've been there a while.

"Then there's Père Fouettard. He keeps to himself, talks to the stout man now and then. No one likes him, really – there's something not right about him. Suits us fine to let him be.

"That's it. Just three grownups, then the rest are kids. Little kids, some of them, as small as six or seven. They all ran away from someplace, or wanted to get away from someplace. I guess maybe I did to, though I don't remember what I was running from. You forget after a while, anyway. It's good work and a warm bed and decent food in the middle of nowhere, so why worry about what you left behind?

"When you're new, like I was, you work painting and polishing. If your work's good, they let you do cutting and pressing. It's hard to keep track of time up there; the days are real short, and they're all the same: fresh snow in the morning, a little sun during the day, the aurora at night. Nothing but snow and hills and a little pine forest around, as far as the eye can see. It's easy to feel like the world just stops turning, like you're frozen in a photograph.

"After a while, though...you start to change. You stop needing to sleep. You don't get hurt as easily. And when you do...

"It was so long ago, I don't even remember how it happened. I just know I was working away at something, and there was an accident, and then my thumb wasn't on my hand any more. Something had cut it clean off. And there it was on the table, like a little worm, not even bleeding. I thought I was gonna die, I was so scared, but it didn't even bleed.

"They made me go to Père Fouettard to get it put back on. He has three boys, and they work the leather goods. And I guess skin must be just like leather to them, because he didn't even blink, he just sewed it right up. Like it happened all the time.

"You know how, when you've seen something strange for the first time, suddenly you see it everywhere? Like you've been blind to this one thing, but now you can see it and you wonder how you ever missed it in the first place? That's what it was like. I'd thought the workshop was safe, that no one really got hurt because everyone was careful, or something like that. But once I got my thumb back on, I saw it all over the place. Big, dangerous equipment being handled by little kids like me. People got hurt all the time. They just bounced back, or got stitched up.

"I don't...I don't remember a lot of what happened after that. Maybe it's because of how I was changing. I know I tried to run away a couple times, but I couldn't. I just ended up back where I started. And then I guess I got used to it, after a while. It wasn't so bad. Sure, the work was hard, but we had fun, too. After that first Christmas, it was like I belonged there, you know? I made friends with the other kids. We'd go sledding and have snowball fights. We didn't have to sleep and we couldn't get hurt. We had all the time in the world to do whatever we wanted to do."

"So why did you leave?" Joe asked, wide-eyed. Alex shot him a sidelong look. He could tell what Joe was thinking.

Carl frowned as he tried to find the words. "Even in a place where nothing changes," he said, "things change. Maybe it was even my fault."

"What do you mean?" asked Katharina.

"I mean…the first time I tried to get away, at the beginning? I had a friend with me. We got out together, but somewhere along the line we got separated. I ended up back at the workshop. She didn't."

"You mean…"

"She got out. I didn't think anything of it at first. What was the point? I figured I'd had my shot, and that was that.   But other people noticed. Fouettard, and the Belsnickel. And they told the stout man, and he got worried."

"I don't understand," said Richard. "He's Santa Claus. He's *good*. Why would he keep people there against their will?"

"He isn't like you think," Carl said. "I think he *thinks* he's good. He says he wants what's best for you, but he doesn't trust you to know what that is. He thinks he's got it all figured out, and the workshop's the best place for a runaway kid. He thinks if you get out, you're only hurting yourself. And whatever he says is best, that's what Fouettard and the Belsnickel do.

"So they kept closer watch on us, and they started picking on anyone they thought was thinking about leaving. And the work got harder, and the days got longer, and after a while I realised: all the things that made me think, hey, maybe it isn't so bad here…they were gone. We were just factory kids, factory kids who couldn't die and couldn't get hurt and couldn't ever leave. I couldn't even remember my parents' names, or where I came from. I wasn't anyone any more.

"I tell you what, you don't know how long forever is until you're looking right at it. It wasn't any one thing that made me realise I couldn't do it any more. It was just one day after another, losing count of the Christmases, knowing I'd never get another present for myself ever again…"

Carl trailed off, his eyes brimming. He went to wipe his nose on the back of his hand, but caught himself, and tugged his sleeve down over the stump of his wrist instead.

"I think I must've been there twenty years," he said, "and one day I realised I wanted to be real again. I knew I couldn't get out as I was. I'd just end up back where I started, if I didn't get caught first. But I could think of one thing that made it to the real world, every time, without fail."

"The presents!" Katharina gasped.

"Exactly," Carl said. "I got a couple of friends to help me. We went through the stout man's things and learned some of his secrets. How the magic worked. How to take a body apart and put it back together again so it lives. We weren't sure it could be done, until we found out…"

He swallowed, suddenly pale. "Père Fouettard's three boys," he said grimly. "They were the key. Fouettard was an ordinary man once, but he was evil. He took in three boys who needed shelter on Christmas Eve, then he killed them and cut them up into pieces. When the stout man visited him that year, and saw what he had done, he made him sew the boys back together so he could bring them back to life. They were the first elves at the workshop – they've been there longer than anyone, but they remembered. They told me what to do so I could come back to life on the other side. Then all my friends had to do was cut me up into pieces like those boys, and hide me and the instructions in presents that were all going to the same place."

"But why Nowhere?" Alex asked. "What's so special about here?"

"That's where my friend was from," Carl said. "The one who got out. I thought maybe, just maybe, there's something about this place that's easier to get to from there, or easier to stay in. It's the only place I know of where someone stayed gone."

Silence hung heavy in the cannery attic as the Liars absorbed Carl's story. Outside, the afternoon sun was starting to make its descent towards the horizon; the light through the windows was warm and gold, though the temperature was dropping. Alex had no idea what time it was, except for the vaguest sense of when sunset was supposed to be.

Maureen pulled her chair forward to get closer to Carl. "I have questions," she said, pushing her glasses up her nose.

Carl shrugged, and tucked the ends of his arms – one hand and one stump – into his armpits for warmth. "Go ahead," he said.

"Our parents," Maureen said. "Why didn't they react to us getting body parts in our presents?"

Carl grinned, the first expression he'd shown that wasn't fear or intense solemnity. "That worked, huh?" he said. "I was hoping it would. See, everyone hits a point where they don't believe any more. They're too old, or just don't have the imagination. But we're still out there, making and delivering presents. It's part of the magic, really: if you don't believe in Santa, the presents just kind of slide off you. You don't question what's in them or how they got under the tree; if someone asks, you just think you bought 'em. It's just a little trick that lets us do our job in peace."

Katharina laughed suddenly. "Of course! Sy Benson!"

Carl looked confused.

"He's our age, but he's Jewish," Katharina explained. "He's never believed in Santa."

"What about me?" said Joe. "I believe. I mean, I never get presents, but I still believe. Why did I think an *ear* was normal?"

Carl frowned, but Alex's stomach dropped. He knew the answer. He *hated* the answer.

"Joe," he said quietly, "the cards. You always believed they were from your dad."

In the sudden, needle-sharp silence, Alex thought he could hear Joe's heart break.

"Joe…" he said, but Joe was already standing, tugging down his sleeves and looking resolutely at anything but his friends.

"Okay," said Joe. "It's been weird. Nice to meet you, Carl, but I gotta put this day to bed. Beans to eat, and all." His eyes met Alex's for a second, shining with dampness he was refusing to let turn into tears. "I gotta say," he said, with a wobbly little smile, "I have had some lousy Christmas Eves, but this one's some kind of prizewinner. I'll see you guys tomorrow."

He turned for the window, but Carl jumped to his feet. "Wait!" he cried. "What did you say?"

"I've got beans to eat," said Joe.

"No, I…after that. What day is it?"

"December 24th, 1945," said Richard. "Christmas Eve."

Carl went white. He clapped his hand to his mouth, forgetting that he had no hand to clap. "Oh no," he said. "Oh, no no no *no*. It's too early. It's not supposed to be now."

"What's the matter?" said Alex.

"You were supposed to find me tomorrow!" Carl

said desperately. "Christmas *Day*. I'm not safe today, not until the sun rises. He'll *find* me!"

"Who?" Alex asked. "Santa? The Belsnickel?"

Carl shook his head. "Worse," he croaked. "*Krampus*."

14

It had started after the first escape. Krampus had always been part of the workshop's operation, but as more of a field officer, out in the world tracking down the children who had not been good enough to earn Christmas presents. He was a legend, a shadowy figure, a beast who sniffed out wrongdoing and who had a very long leash when it came to meting out punishment. The Belsnickel set your hair on end; Père Fouettard made your stomach clench; but only Krampus filled you with actual fear.

After the Belsnickel and Fouettard failed to find the escapee, Krampus came back to the workshop. He would stalk around the perimeter, leaving deep hoofprints in the snow, and when the elves asked what he was there for they were told, simply, "security". He would watch them file back to the dormitories at the end of the working day, and at night, they would see him making his circuits around the building in the light of the aurora. Every day, there would be a fresh set of hoofprints in the snow, marking the path from the dorm-itories to the little train station, and after a while the elves were too afraid even to stroll down to the station to chat with the affable train conductor, Rudy.

The snowball fights and sledding stopped. The hollows between the pines, cherished semi-private places to spend time with friends, emptied out as the elves felt ever more as though they could see those glittering eyes between the trees, or hear the soft crunch of goat hooves in the snow-soaked carpet of pine needles. The elves at the workshop had always worked hard, but now, with Krampus around, the amiable hum of activity became a tense silence of fear, interrupted only by the sounds of the cutters and pressers stamping their punctuation into the air, and the clacking and swishing of screwdrivers and paintbrushes at work.

As soon as life at the workshop stopped being fun, more of the elves tried to leave.

They were told that Krampus was under strict instructions not to hurt them. There would have been no point: actually leaving the workshop was near-impossible thanks to the strange pocket of reality it was tucked into, and the stout man – Father Christmas – insisted that no one really *wanted* to leave; they just got rattled and made rash decisions. Why punish someone for a mistake they didn't mean, with no real consequences?

The thing was, when you could bounce back from any injury and heal from any wound, it was really hard to tell whether Krampus was sticking to his instructions. The would-be-escapees he brought back *looked* fine, if scareder and quieter than usual. But bruises faded quickly at the workshop; broken bones knitted themselves back together; and even an arm sliced right off in a cutter accident could be sewn back on, good as new, by Fouettard and his boys.

Not every child Krampus brought back in his sack was an escaped elf. It had soon become clear that Krampus was out recruiting as well. The train still went out to pick up runaways in search of jobs, but less and less often, and it came back less and less full. Somewhere along the line, it seemed as though Krampus was told that an eternity at the workshop was another lump of coal he could add to his bag of punishments for bad children, and he used it gleefully.

The changes had all fed off each other, from that very first successful escape. The more Krampus was around, the worse the workshop got. The worse the workshop got, the more elves tried to leave. The more elves tried to leave, the more power Krampus had. And the more of his recruits that he brought back in his sack, rebellious and stubborn as they already were, the worse it got and the more elves tried to escape. The stout man turned a blind eye, and Krampus got more and more inventive in his hunts and punishments for wayward elves.

"He's a monster," Carl said, shuddering. "He'll cut me up into pieces just to watch me put myself back together again. He'll beat me and stuff me in his sack. He'll take me back, and then I'll be one of *them* – one of the ones that can't be trusted. I'll be chained to my workbench and I'll never eat or sleep or leave my station again. You have to help me."

"What happens," Maureen asked, "if we can keep him off you until Christmas morning?"

"I change back, I think," Carl said. "I become a boy again. And then, as long as I'm good, Krampus and Fouettard and the Belsnickel can't touch me."

"You *think*?" Maureen demanded. "Do you have proof? Have you tested your theory?"

Carl swallowed. "It's a guess," he said, "but I think it's a good one. Look, almost no one gets away what doesn't get caught again. But a few – a very few – have. Just two or three, out of all the ones who've tried. But if they stay away past Christmas…I don't know if it's a rule or if Krampus just loses interest. Maybe he figures after that point it's not worth the trouble. It's all I've got to go on, but I've seen it happen. I can promise you that."

They decided to hide Carl in the Red House. Richard wanted to stand and fight, but Alex and Katharina were still too shaken from their encounter with Julian, and Maureen and Joe were about as useful in a scrap as wet noodles. As for Carl, well, he only had one hand to work with. Hiding was the only option, and the Red House was the only place that made sense: it was the only place in Nowhere that didn't celebrate Christmas. It was neutral ground.

"I don't know," said Joe, his joking smirk not quite as confident as normal. "Semitic Switzerland still got a torso".

Still, it was the best idea they had. The setting sun was behind them as they trudged up Buckingham Bluffs, the temperature dropping rapidly so that the sweat of the steep hike ran down their necks in icy little rivulets. They left their bikes behind; Katharina's was still at the meadow, and neither Carl nor Joe had one to ride in the first place. Katharina and Carl walked side-by-side, unconsciously balancing each other out with two good hands between them.

Sy's parents were not home, which was a relief. They usually went out on Christmas Eve, Sy explained cheerfully, sometimes all the way to Santa Mira to enjoy the lights and socialise with the handful of other Jewish families in the area. Richard asked why Sy wasn't with them.

"Never really liked Chinese food," Sy said with a shrug.

That gave the Liars the run of the Red House, and plenty of places to try to hide Carl. Sy led them back, past the cavernous living room and the staircase that curved up to the upper floors, past the kitchen with its view into the dense woods, and through the hallway that seemed to mark exactly where the Bensons' time, money, or enthusiasm for the renovations had simply run out. Within the space of a few steps, the new hardwood flooring gave way to old, creaking boards; the Bensons' tasteful striped wallpaper stopped abruptly as it met peeling, faded florals; and the tall, light-welcoming windows the Bensons favoured shrank down into the squat arches of the older structure. The house was even bigger than Alex had guessed from the outside, and he began to lose track of which direction was lake and which direction was mountainside as Sy led them deeper and deeper into the rotting, sun-pinked old wing.

They settled on a room with rot-black beams criss-crossing a low ceiling, and walls lined with shelves that sagged ponderously in the middle. A small door with an old-fashioned latch led onto a narrow path into the woods, while, at the back, part of the wall had crumbled away completely, revealing a deep fissure in the mountain behind that exhaled a cool, stale-smelling breeze if you stood right in front of it.

"This is the creepiest room I've ever seen," Joe said with a shudder.

"Thanks," Sy answered with his easy smile. "No one's been in it for years. Well, except me when I get really bored. If you need to get out in a hurry, the path out that door will take you up the top of the bluffs in a windy sort of way. Whatever you do, don't go into the caves."

"Why?" asked Carl. "What's in the caves?"

Sy just raised a cheeky eyebrow, and left them to their business.

It was getting dark quickly. The sun was setting behind a ridge of mountain and the dense forest outside, and the cool light in the abandoned room turned an ashy grey. Outside, snow was falling again; Alex could see the speckling of white against the anaemic light in the windows, and a thin column of flakes drifted lazily down into a corner of the room from a hole in the ceiling.

The only sources of light inside were a bare lightbulb on a wire near the cave entrance, and a couple of bulky handheld flashlights Sy had left them. They put one of these on the floor and shielded it with some old chairs, nervous about the dark but afraid of giving away their presence to anyone outside. Then they settled in to wait.

Despite their nerves and the rising cold, the Liars found themselves adjusting to the situation quickly. After all, this wasn't so dissimilar to hiding out in the cannery attic after shaking off Julian and his goons, or creeping into the woods together when Joe's mother got in one of her moods and came shouting for him to do some mundane thing that didn't matter. Waiting out the night against a supernatural monster in an abandoned wing of the Red House wasn't so different as all that, it turned out.

It was the weird sense of familiarity that stopped Alex from realising, as he joined in the whispered jokes and storytelling, that Carl was no longer with the group huddled around the flashlight. He looked around, suddenly afraid that somehow Krampus had got in and stolen him away without any of them noticing, but he quickly spotted him by the entrance to the caves, staring into the darkness under the sickly glow of that one bare lightbulb. Alex got up and went over to him.

"I don't think he's getting in that way," Alex said. Carl jumped a little at the sound of his voice.

"Why not?" Carl asked. "Where do they go?"

"No one really knows," Alex said. The caves under Mount Konocti were a Lake County legend; a fraction of the system of volcanic fissures had been explored, and a few were safe to hang out in if you didn't mind the dark. The rest, though…not all of the stories of people going missing in the caves were legends. Two of the older kids from school had disappeared just last year; they had left their friends at the entrance of one of the caves and ventured inside on a dare, and one hadn't been seen since. The other had been found floating in the middle of Clear Lake, his body swollen like an over-stuffed doll. Alex didn't think there was any way a creature like Krampus could find them through the caves, even if he was supernatural.

"You okay?" Alex asked Carl. Even with the lukewarm reassurance about the caves, Carl still looked pale and pinched, staring absently into the fissure in the rock. Alex noticed that he was tugging at the sleeve around his truncated wrist, shifting the shirt cuff as though he couldn't get it to sit right.

"I was gonna learn to whittle," Carl said. "There was a guy in…" he frowned, trying to remember. "Must've been Calistoga, I think. He made little birds and things out of bits of wood. I had this idea of hopping a boxcar to somewhere exciting, and whittling as I went. I never got to do it at the workshop. I did painting and sewing, mostly, not woodworking. I figured if I managed to get out, I'd finally learn. Just a little thing to keep me going, you know?" He looked down at the shirt cuff, picking at a thread that wasn't really loose. "I know I should be scared right now, or even grateful you guys are doing so much for me, but all I can think is…I could get through all this, even Krampus, and I'll still never be able to whittle."

Alex took a breath. "My dad…" he began, then paused. He wasn't sure if he was about to say something necessary or commit a terrible betrayal. He thought it might be both. "My dad lost most of his hand in the war," he said finally.

Tony looked at him. "The Great War?"

Alex actually laughed a little. "Yeah, there's, uh, been another one since. It only ended this year."

"Oh. Wow."

"Anyway, he, uh, he was a combat medic. Not a doctor – that's different – but someone who could help out the wounded quickly, you know? Get them patched up just enough that they didn't die on the way to the real doctors. My mom says he was really good at it."

Images of his dad gently wrapping Katharina's arm swam into Alex's mind. He swallowed down the sudden tightness in his throat. "He doesn't really talk about what happened, but we were told he was trying to help someone, and he was shot. They…they kept telling us it could have been worse. I know it could've. At least he came home, right? They gave him a medal and everything.

"He, uh…he used to play guitar. Not professionally or anything. Actually he wasn't even that good. But it was something he really enjoyed, especially around Christmas. He'd play, and we'd sing carols. My mom keeps telling me he's been through a lot, and he'll come back to us – *really* come back to us – in his own time, but I keep thinking, *'If he could just pick up a guitar again'*…I don't know. Maybe he'd come back faster."

The two boys looked at each other. Alex had a feeling he ought to say something else; that there was more Carl needed to hear. But before he could say anything, there was a sudden crash from outside, and a voice rang harshly through the night.

"Hey, losers! I know you're in there! In there with your Nazi friend!"

It was Julian.

15

Far below the Red House, where the tracks of the abandoned railroad slid into the icy waters of Clear Lake, a figure emerged from the water.

If you believed in werewolves, you might have mistaken it for one at first. The figure had thick, ropy fur, broad shoulders, and a long, doglike face with a predator's teeth. But werewolves were not supposed to have hooves that clicked on the pebbles of the lakeshore like an unloaded gun trying to fire. Werewolves were not supposed to have horns that curved around the listening ears and came to wicked points alongside the sharp, bristled cheeks. Werewolves did not have slender, forked tongues that tasted the air in quick, darting flicks.

The creature stood upright, shook the water from its pelt, and breathed in the chill, Nowhere air.

It knew exactly what it was looking for, and it smelled traces of it on the breeze, in the earth, along the sides of buildings. The scent was scattered, broken into too many pieces, their trails weaving into town and criss-crossing like the strands of a spider's web. The creature snarled, its breath steaming between its pointed teeth to billow in the frigid air.

The number of trails for a single target was a question mark, but the creature barely hesitated. Keeping to the shadows, it followed one thread after another, peering in windows and sniffing at doors, tasting the pieces of what it wanted but never quite finding the whole. Sometimes the trails came together for a while, and it followed a bundle of them to an old building near the lake, where, up a rickety fire escape and through a broken window, the trail grew strong and hot in a dusty attic, surrounded by old furniture and stacks of crates. This place had more than just the scent of the creature's target; it had a charge in the air, acid and electric, that pricked at the inside of the creature's nose and made the scent it was tracking turn fuzzy and dull. Where the trail had gone next, the creature could not tell.

The creature backtracked, following an older thread to a barren patch of land with scrubby grass and a shallow pond. An abandoned bicycle lay in the grass near the road, and scattered around were the remnants of children playing: toy arrows lost to the grass, a wooden hobby-horse with its pole snapped off; a crushed cowboy hat sitting sadly in the muddy pond. Two wisps of scent converged here; one of them the one the creature had followed from the attic, where everything went dull, and another that split off into the woods at the far end of the scrubby clearing. Every other thread the creature had followed flowed into the bundle that went sour in the attic, but this one… this one was clear, and bright, and delicious with expectation. The creature set its ears back, and followed the scent into the trees.

There was little purpose to the trail. It weaved and meandered, making stops at little clues to an aimless, sometimes cruel life. Here was a sagging couch teetering on the hillside, next to the remnants of a fire pit and a tumble of old magazines. There was a pile of bones, some cat, some squirrel, some maybe a dog, some with the skin still on them. Over in the shade of a towering pine was a little box with a toy gun – the kind that shot round metal pellets that could take an eye out – and an empty space just big enough for a pocket knife. The very tip of a little finger, cut to just below where the nail started, was in the dirt next to the box. The scent on it was as strong as a lit cigar.

The trail continued up the hill in a lazy, swinging arc, until it seemed to pool and spread at a spot just a few feet back from the road that climbed up the mountain. Whatever had made its aimless way to this place had stopped for a while, waiting for something. The creature's nostrils flared; the road itself had the same tart, electric smell as the abandoned attic. The scent the creature was tracking followed in the electric trail's wake, its brightness dulled a little, but not snuffed out. Crouching low to the side of the road, the creature stalked up the mountain, following the smell of its prey, ears stiff and alert to the sounds of muffled voices carried through the pines from the far-off wing of a red, rotting house.

There were people up in front of that rotting wing, people about the same size and shape as the creature's quarry. But it was not the figures themselves that held the scent: that was in something smaller, something that the largest of the people was holding in the air, waving at the others with a sneer and a taunt. It was too small; it was incomplete. It was not what the creature was here for.

That tingling, electric smell was thick in the air, and it was muffling the creature's senses. The creature shook its head, sucking in cold air through its wicked teeth, holding back its urge to snarl so that it could stay, unseen and unheard, in the shadows. The figure holding the object with the scent was shouting something, and the creature pricked its ears to hear.

"*...come in there and take the rest of him, piece by piece...*"

Suddenly the creature understood. Invisible against the hollows of the trees, black fur on black shadows, it crept towards the crumbling wing of the Red House. The figures kept shouting, oblivious to the creature's approach. Behind them, the house itself seemed to pulse with that same electric smell, sharp in the creature's ears like the whine of mosquitos, acerbic as vinegar.

In the space between the pines, where trees met mountainside and volcanic rock punched skyward out of the earth, the creature found a crack between two great slabs of basalt. Damp, stale air oozed out of the cave and sank into the carpet of pine needles at its entrance. The creature flicked out its forked tongue, sensing, tasting, feeling that electric thrum on its tastebuds.

The creature smiled, thin black lips peeling back over jagged teeth. These caves had been made for creatures like him.

Julian had Sy Benson by the neck, and the crazed glint in his eye said that he would choke him out right there in front of the Red House without a second thought. Alex's heart leapt into his chest as he saw the mountain of a boy, clutching Sy in one hand like a doll with the stuffing gone out of it, throwing Carl's missing hand up and down like a baseball in the other. Maureen, Joe, and Richard almost bumped into him as they came running out of the Red House. Katharina had heard Julian's voice and frozen right to the spot in the back of the dilapidated room, clutching at Carl and begging him not to leave her alone.

"That's ours," Alex said, too scared to say anything else.

"What, this?" Julian sneered, giving the hand a final toss before dropping it to the ground. "Or," he said, whipping his knife out of his pocket and jabbing it towards Sy's heaving chest, "*this*?"

"Let him go!" Maureen yelled, her voice a brave, futile squeak.

"On Christmas Eve?" Julian said cruelly. "Nah,

that wouldn't be Christian. He's a *Jew*. They killed Jesus. Too many of his kind around and there's no point having Christmas at all. I should do everyone a favour and make one less of him in the world, shouldn't I?"

Alex shook his head, numbly. His tongue felt like a slab of lard in his mouth and he wasn't sure if he was hearing the stupidest or the most terrifying speech of his life.

Julian's eyes flicked from Alex, to Joe, to Richard, to Maureen. Alex thought he could actually see him counting, as though the numbers were flicking across his big, meaty head and not quite adding up. Julian grinned cruelly.

"Where's your Nazi friend?" he asked. "You hiding her from me? You gonna be traitors to the US of A? Bring her out, I'll show you what a real American does."

"Jesus Christ!" yelled Joe, with such exasperation Julian actually hesitated.

"You can't have it both ways, idiot," Joe cried. "You gotta pick one. Do you hate Jews, or do you hate Nazis?"

Julian's eyes bulged with rage. He tightened his grip on Sy's collar, and Sy's face started to go purple. Maureen took a step towards him, but Alex flung out his arm to stop her. He had no idea what Julian was going to do next, and that scared him more than the knife glinting in the low moonlight.

"I should cut you all into pieces," Julian hissed, flecks of spit flying from his mouth. "Jew boy.

Nazi Kraut. Four-eyed freak. I've been working on the piece of your friend you gave me."

He kicked the hand towards the Liars, and Alex saw with a swell of nausea that the tip of the little finger was gone, crudely sawn off just below the nail bed.

Julian pointed the knife at the wing of the Red House. "I should come in there and take the rest of him, piece by piece," he said. Even in the dark, his pupils were pinpricks in his pale eyes. Sy gasped for breath.

Alex felt Richard snap. He had felt it once before, a long time ago, when they had been walking downtown and seen a couple of Okie boys messing with Richard's sister. Richard was a kind kid, a gentle giant, a master at taking it all in and pushing it down, and down, and down beneath an easy smile and a friendly word. When Richard snapped was the only time Alex had ever seen it all come back up again, and he recognised the rising tide of rage just soon enough to pull Maureen and Joe out of the way.

Richard dove for Julian with an inhuman roar. Julian was bigger, but Richard was *done*. This wasn't a fight: it was divine retribution, revenge for hurting Sy, for threatening his friends, and – worst of all – for injuring Katharina when he hadn't been there to protect her. Richard's fists were a whirlwind: he drove at Julian non-stop, bellowing with rage, taking slashes in the arms from the pocket knife but raining blows down anyway.

Even under the hail of Richard's fists, Julian

never lost his grip on Sy's collar. Sy was jerked back and forth, his feet scrabbling for grip in the pine needles, his eyes bulging.

"He's gonna kill him!" cried Joe. He and Alex sprinted forwards and grabbed Sy by the shoulders, trying to pull him free; Maureen pushed in between them and bit down hard on Julian's clenched fist. That finally did it; Julian howled and his fist popped open, and Joe, Alex, Sy and Maureen tumbled backwards into the snow-speckled dirt, Sy coughing up deep, heaving breaths. Their balance broken, Julian and Richard flailed for a moment, tangled up in each other's flying fists, before falling out of sight down the hill, crashing through the undergrowth as they rolled into the deep of the woods.

"We should go after them," Alex said, his heart pounding.

"No, thank you," wheezed Sy, as he got painfully to his feet. His breath came in whistling gasps, but at least his face was no longer purple. "I'm out. I didn't ask to get choked to death for Christmas."

"You didn't ask for *anything* for Christmas," Joe said acidly.

Alex yanked at Joe's arm. "Please, Sy," he said. "We need you. Without Richard, there aren't enough of us to fight..."

From inside the house, Katharina screamed.

16

"W-what the hell is *that*?" Sy stammered.

Some tiny part of Alex's brain – the part that still refused to believe that any of this was real, even after everything he had seen – recognised that Sy had run right into the house with them at the sound of Katharina's scream, even after the beating he'd taken from Julian. That tiny part of Alex's brain appreciated that, a lot.

A much bigger part of Alex's brain was flooded with terror at the scene inside the Red House.

Katharina clung to a baluster under one of the sagging shelves, her elbow and leg hooked desperately around it for grip. Her other hand, stretched so taut her arm looked about to come out of its socket, gripped Carl's hand like a vice. Carl was strung out like Christmas bunting, pulled between Katharina's straining grip, and the claws that were sunk into his leg from the creature at the mouth of the cave. Krampus had come to collect.

Alex had never seen anything so terrifying. The creature was seven feet tall at least, covered in thick, black fur, with pitch-black eyes and a blood-red tongue that darted between its lips as it pulled at Carl's leg. The hands ended in vicious claws; the legs, thick and muscular, came to cold grey hooves that struck sparks off the cave floor as Krampus threw his weight into the terrible tug-of-war. The creature's head was lowered like an ox at the yoke and its breath poured into the room in bilious clouds. Its red-rimmed nostrils flared under a flat, leathery nose. It growled as it pulled at Carl's leg, and long, jagged fangs glinted in the sickly light of the bare bulb.

A tripping, receding thudding told Alex that Sy was escaping, sprinting out of the rotted wing and back towards the renovated part of the Red House. He must be hoping it was safe there. Alex vaguely hoped he was right.

Carl screamed shrilly. The loose fabric of Richard's oversized pants had saved him; Krampus had clawfuls of fabric instead of chunks of Carl's flesh. But Krampus was clearly realising his mistake, scrabbling for better purchase, and meanwhile Alex could see an awful pink seam opening up at Carl's wrist, where Katharina's grip was pulling at the fresh scar…

"Hey!" he yelled. "Leave him alone!"

This is not my day for trash talk, Alex thought, as Krampus turned his horrible, horned head to look at him. *First Julian, now Krampus. I'm gonna have to change some things when I tell people about tonight.*

He didn't dare say *If I survive*, even to himself.

The creature sucked in an awful, hissing breath, forked tongue flashing between the razor-sharp shards of its teeth. *This is it*, Alex thought. *We're all dead. And the best I could come up with was "Leave him alone!"*

But the momentary distraction was enough. Carl struck out with his other leg and kicked Krampus viciously in the shoulder. The leg of his pants tore, the claws loosened for just a moment, and Carl wrenched his leg loose and scrambled over to Katharina, leaving Krampus holding handfuls of ragged fabric.

Carl grabbed Katharina by the hand and sprinted over to the other Liars, his ragged pants leg flapping as he ran. Alex and Maureen caught them, and the four Liars and Carl clung to each other, trembling, too frightened to move, as Krampus shook his head and turned his snarling face to them.

His breath billowed from his mouth, clouds of sickly yellow mist in the light of the bare bulb. He stamped his hoof on the floor, splinters flying up from the rotting boards. When he spoke, his voice was like ice scraping across rocks on the bottom of a river.

"That one is mine," he said, pointing one wicked claw at Carl.

"You can't have him!" Maureen said shrilly.

Krampus licked his lips. "Then I shall have you all," he said.

He lunged for them, and they scattered. Fear made them quick on their feet, and all five of them were able to stay just clear of the slashing claws. Alex stumbled into the barricade they had used to hide the flashlight; he felt Krampus miss his ankle by a hair, and he grabbed at the heavy flashlight and swung it wildly behind him. It hit the creature's shoulder with a solid, meaty thump. The weight of it was too much, and Alex was pulled all the way around with the momentum of his swing, and once again Krampus' slashing claws missed him by barely an inch. He staggered backwards, grabbing at Joe and pulling him out of the way as Krampus wheeled and swung his horns at where Joe had been a second before.

The creature was herding them towards the wall. They were managing to stay out of his way, but every time they dodged, they took a step back, closing back in from where they had scattered. Alex dared a glance at the little door, still un-latched, but Krampus was smarter than that. He had seen them come in that way, and with each swipe of his claws he herded them towards the opposite corner, away from their only escape. Their only escape except...

Alex's heart beat wildly in his throat. He was terrified, almost more frightened of what he was about to do than of the hideous creature in front of him, but it was their only option. He took a deep breath, stepped backwards, waited for Krampus to get just the right distance away.

"Break!" he screamed.

Somehow, the others understood. Joe and Mau-reen went left; Alex, Katharina and Carl went right, and they spilled around Krampus and sprinted for the cave. The heavy flashlight did almost nothing against the pitch black of the cave, but Alex didn't care. His feet skidded on the slick stone, he flailed his arms, the light of the flashlight skittering wildly off hanging stalactites, and he sprinted on, tugging Katharina behind him, plunging into the heart of the mountain.

Within a few minutes, it seemed as though they had been in the caves for hours, running from tunnel to tunnel, the flashlight bouncing on the rock in front of them and the sound of Krampus' hooves never far behind.   Almost immediately, Alex assumed they were lost; one turn and the faint hint of light from the bulb at the entrance was gone, one more and he could no longer remember how many turns they had taken.   He gripped tightly to Katharina's hand, slick and clammy with sweat, and ran, stumbling in the darkness, praying they wouldn't hit a dead end. The thought of the two missing boys, one floating face-down in the lake, swam horribly into his mind. They would never make it out alive. Krampus would catch them and tear them all to pieces, or they would be swallowed by the mountain, never to be seen again.

"Alex!" Maureen cried breathlessly. "We have to get out of here. There's sulphur in these caves – we'll suffocate!"

That was why his head was swimming, why his eyes felt too big in their sockets, why it felt like the cold hard rock below was sagging and bouncing under his feet. The beam of the flashlight caught a slick seam of obsidian, and oily rainbows danced in front of Alex's eyes as the light scattered off the rock. The sudden spray of colour disoriented him and he tripped, crashing hard to his knees on the damp stone floor.

The others stumbled into him, losing their footing in turn and tumbling to the ground. Maureen felt for his sleeve and clutched it in a tight, panicked grip.

"We're never gonna get out of here," Joe wheezed. "We'll be running around these caves forever. Remember all those stories about ghosts in the caves? Turns out they aren't ghosts, they're just us. We're ghosts already and we just don't know it yet…"

"Shut up!" Katharina cried shrilly, and Joe shut up.

They could still hear Krampus' hooves scraping on the rock, but they were quieter, maybe further away. Or maybe they weren't; maybe it was just the twists and turns in the passages muffling the sound, and any second now he would come crashing through and be on top of them…

Carl was the only one who hadn't fallen. In the scattered light of the dropped flashlight Alex could see him, staring down a pitch-black passageway, rainbows splattered on his chalk-white face.

"I can get us out," he said.

Alex crawled over to Carl and pulled himself painfully to his feet. "How do you know?" he asked, his head still swimming.

"The same way *he* does," Carl said, and Alex

knew he meant the scrabbling of Krampus' hooves behind them. "It's in me, somehow. In my seams. These caves were made for creatures like us."

Carl made Alex take his hand and turn off the flashlight. Katharina started crying with fear; Joe's breaths were shallow and hysterical. They all trembled like leaves in the wind as, strung out like a chain of paper people, they followed Carl hand-in-hand through the suffocating black. The hoof-falls behind them got closer, then farther away, then closer again, echoing off the rock and sounding everywhere and nowhere at once. Alex stumbled, his legs like jelly and his head swimming, but Carl yanked him forwards, and he pulled on Katharina, and behind him he felt Katharina tug Joe forwards and Joe grab at Maureen, and he wondered if there were more of them, more ghosts-to-be, or maybe ghosts-that-already-were, a chain of them going down and down and down into the mountain.

Even the darkness seemed to split and come apart in the grip of his terror, a strip of silvery grey cracking down the middle of the black. Only the split wasn't in his head, he realised as it got bigger: it was a split in the rock, a crack between two walls of basalt, and the silver was moonlight and the grey was snow, and Carl gave him a final pull forward and he burst through the gap, and air, glorious air, streamed into his lungs, icy cold and wet with falling snow. The moon was high now, streaming down through the pines and bright as a thousand-watt lamp, reflected in the dusty windows of the broken wing of the Red House.

All that time in the caves, and they had got nearly nowhere at all – just run around in circles in the belly of the mountain.

They had no time to catch their breath. The sound of scraping hooves was getting louder again, echoing off the stone and out into the open air. Alex thought he saw the moonlight glinting off Krampus' obsidian-black eyes as he scrambled backwards and to his feet.

Maureen started running back towards the front of the Red House, but Alex grabbed her sleeve. "No!" he cried. "We can't lead him to Sy!"

There was no time to argue, and no one wanted to. This was their fight – theirs and Carl's. There was only one way left to go.

17

The path up to the top of Buckingham Bluffs was winding and steep. The higher they climbed, the narrower the path got, the ground spilling away on either side in ever-steeper slopes and down into the darkness of the woods. They scrambled and stumbled, running as fast as they could, but behind them Krampus was faster, his goat-hooves quick and sure on the slippery rock. They didn't dare look back, but they knew he would catch them.

Suddenly the ground in front of them flattened out and poured away down the mountain. They had reached the top. The highest point of Buckingham Bluffs was a narrow ridge of bare shale, grey and slick as a sheet of ice, and on any other night the view over the treetops clear down to the moon-spackled lake would have been breathtaking. But the ridge only lasted a few feet before dropping away into a sheer cliff and a suicidal drop into the carpet of pines far below.

Finally, they had no choice but to turn and face

their pursuer.

Krampus took the sheer scramble up to the ridge like it was nothing. The frigid wind whipped at his fur and made the Liars clutch at each other for balance, but he was sure-footed, one hoof squarely in front of the other as he slowed to stare hungrily at his prey.

"I will take you," Krampus hissed, his forked tongue darting around his lips. "I will take all of you. Bad children must be punished."

There was nowhere left to go. The sides of Buckingham Bluffs fell steeply away beneath them in all directions except the one from which Krampus was coming. On one side was sheer cliff, a steep drop into nothingness; on the other, the forest was so dense and dark that they could not see where the ground was. There was no escape route that wouldn't get them lost in the caves, or broken at the bottom of a rock face.

Carl turned to the others with moonlight shining off the in his eyes. "You should just let him take me," he whispered.

"Like hell we will," Joe retorted, and the Liars spread out in front of Carl and faced Krampus down.

The creature licked his lips, the forked tongue a strip of bloody red against the white of his teeth. "I'll take you all," he said, his breath fogging the air. "One by—"

A baseball flew out of nowhere, and hit Krampus square in the face.

Time seemed to slow to a standstill as the baseball bounced off the leathery cheek, hit

Krampus' shoulder, and thudded to the ground. Alex thought he felt his heart stop completely. Krampus crouched, picked up the ball, and held it to his nose, inhaling deeply. He grinned his terrible grin, and Alex saw a thin rim of dark blood at the base of his back teeth.

"Such bad children," Krampus said. "All the more for me to take…"

The second baseball impaled itself on Krampus' horn.

Alex couldn't help himself. He laughed. It started in his chest, in the place where his heart had forgotten to beat, and swelled into his stomach and up through his throat, and he laughed and laughed and laughed so hard he thought his ribs were going to crack.

As if his laugh had been a signal, the children of Nowhere swarmed out of the trees and up onto the ridge.

Freddie Maas brandished his bat, a satchel full of baseballs bouncing off his hip. Sy Benson aimed his toy rifle and fired, pellet after pellet thudding like hailstones into Krampus' thick fur. Sissy Lohengrin and Emma Cagliostro came screaming out of the woods, swinging wooden rulers like battle axes, and Tommy Waid, shrieking like a banshee, carried little Kyle Brenner with his cowboy boots on his shoulders, handing pebbles up so Kyle could take devastating aim with his slingshot. Eugene Brady had his bow and arrows from camp. Isobel Winter held a riding crop in one hand and swung an iron stirrup like a flail in the other. Callum Carnegie had nothing but his fists, but he knew how to use them. And behind them all came Richard, sweaty and dirt-streaked, his pants torn at the knee, with Julian Brenner's pocketknife clutched in his fist.

"You're alive!" Katharina shrieked, and as the swarm of children surged towards Krampus, she pushed through them to Richard and threw her arms around him.

"And I brought help," Richard said fiercely.

If the other kids were scared at the sight of Krampus, it didn't slow them down. Freddie pitched and thwacked another baseball, smacking it into the meat of Krampus' chest; a few steps later, he was too close to pitch and just laid in with the bat instead. Tommy kept little Kyle out of reach of Krampus' long arms and sharp claws, but Kyle's aim with his slingshot was unerring, and rock after rock slammed into the predatory face. The girls ducked and weaved under Krampus' swinging arms and kicking hooves, and laid into him with their rulers and riding crop. Sy braced his rifle against his chest and fired, again and again, every pellet finding its mark.

It was over in minutes. Under the weight of fifteen children screaming for their pound of flesh, Krampus crashed to his knees, his hooves skidding out from under him. Isobel, Sissy, and Emma grabbed one arm and held it firm; Tommy and Eugene held fast to the other. Freddie stuck a baseball on Krampus' other horn, just to keep things even. The Liars swallowed the last of their fear and lined up in front of Krampus, looking down at the leathery face bruised from the baseballs and pock-marked with rifle pellets.

Krampus stared up at them, his black eyes still flashing with pride. "You are all bad children," he growled, the words mushy in his bruised mouth. "I will have all of you for Christmas!"

"Oh, shut *up*!" Richard said.

If anything, Krampus was more surprised at that than at being defeated by an army of children. Even held to his knees, Krampus was only an inch or two shorter than Richard, but Richard made even that small difference count, drawing himself up to his fullest height and staring down at Krampus with fire in his eyes.

"You're a bully," Richard said. "That's all you are. You look for any little thing you can find to make someone else seem worse than you, then you use it as an excuse to mess with them. And you know what?"

He stuck the point of Julian's pocketknife under the hairy chin and tilted Krampus' snarling face up towards his. "I *hate* bullies," Richard said.

Krampus spat. "I know bad children!" he said. "And bad children must be punished!"

Richard grabbed a handful of Krampus' hair and pulled his head sharply back. They were nose to nose, so close that the clouds of their breath mingled into a single column, and Richard was *mad*.

"We put a kid back together," Richard snapped. "We spent the whole of Christmas Eve hunting down his pieces, and we *helped* each other, and we *fixed* him. And when we found out he was still in danger, we *protected* him. Some weird little elf kid none of us had ever met, who just wanted to be a boy again. If that makes us bad, then I don't care about being good."

A murmur of assent rippled around the other children. Tommy cupped his hand to his mouth and whooped. Krampus glared at Richard with bulging, furious eyes. He was like a trapped coyote, backed into a corner and vicious, and, as Alex looked into those frantic black eyes, he realised something else.

Krampus was scared.

"Hey Carl," Alex said. "Come over here."

Carl worked his way through the crowd of kids to Krampus. His face was moon-white and his brown eyes were wide as dinner plates, but he took a deep breath and planted himself firmly between Alex and Richard.

"You know him best," Alex said. "What should we do with him?"

Clenching his one fist, Carl took a deep breath. "There are no bad children here," he said. "He has no power over us. We take him back down to the lake. Then we send him home."

There was only one safe route back down Buckingham Bluffs, so they all took it, Krampus included. They made a strange procession through the woods, moving almost single-file down the narrow path, to all appearances led by the hulking beast in front...except that his hands were tightly bound with the belt of Isobel Winter's dressing gown and Richard was pointing Julian's pocket knife into the small of his back. The rest of the children strung out behind as they made their way down the winding path, slipping occasionally on loose pine needles.

Alex sidestepped past a couple of the girls to get level with Sy Benson. "Thanks for coming back," he said. "You didn't have to."

"Sure I did," Sy said amiably. The neck of his sweater was stretched and mangled where Julian had gripped it, and the lapels of his shirt were crumpled like discarded notepaper. Alex thought he could see a line of bruises swelling to life around Sy's neck, but it was hard to tell in the deep shadows.

"Look," Sy said, "I'm pretty used to being beat up on because I'm Jewish. Don't like it, but I'm used to it. I'm much less used to anyone helping me out. So when I looked back out the window and saw you guys getting chased up the Bluffs by..."

"Krampus?" Alex offered.

"It is still *so* weird to say it out loud. Yes, Krampus. Anyway, I couldn't just sit by. Besides" – he smiled wryly – "Richard got the whole town involved. Didn't want to be left out of the fun, you know?"

How Richard had got the knife away from Julian and escaped, no one knew; Richard was too focused on Krampus to tell the story. But Alex pieced together from the other kids what had happened next. He must have rescued Katharina's bike from the edge of the meadow and ridden it into town, pedalling as he had never pedalled before, the dirt and rotten pine needles of his tumble down the mountain clinging to him as he went. He had started with Tommy Waid, of all people, knowing that Ellen Waid loved him for being kind to her son, and that she would give him anything he needed in an emergency even if he looked like he'd gone through a washing machine backwards.

What he had needed was a phone.

He had called every kid on the map, interrupting bedtimes and evening carol singing and the Christmas Eve radio broadcasts to raise up an army out of every kid who had got a foot or an eyeball or a limb in their Christmas presents. *Meet me at the foot of the Bluffs,* he had said, *and bring a weapon, because Krampus is coming and he's out for our blood. And by the way,* he'd added, to the handful of kids – Isobel, Callum, Emma – who'd wanted nothing more to do with the whole thing, *those body parts you found are a boy now, and he's in danger. So you're involved whether you like it or not.*

That strange magic that worked on parents and nonbelievers must have kept working, because the kids had slipped out of their windows or even walked right out their front doors, and their parents had been none the wiser. And so the rag-tag army had made their way up the Bluffs, Richard their mud-spattered commander, Julian's confiscated pocketknife their banner.

"And then," said Freddie, bringing Alex all the way up to date, "I hit Krampus in the face with a baseball."

As they came out of the forest outside the wing at the back of the Red House, Krampus stopped short, hissing as the pocketknife dug into his back.

"You have got to be *kidding* me," sighed Joe.

Julian was in the clearing again. He looked even worse than Richard. His clothes were torn, scraped knees and bloody elbows poking through ragged fabric. His face was scratched from tumbling through the woods, and his hair stuck straight up from his head, crusted into wild spikes with mud and melted snow. His eyes were wild – wilder, even, than Krampus' – and flecks of spittle sprayed from his mouth as he shrieked at the descending children.

"I'll kill you!" he screamed. "I'll kill you all! I'll cut you into little pieces and…"

The words died in his throat as he saw Krampus. For a second his mouth just worked, up and down and open and closed like a fish pulled from the lake. Alex thought, with a surprising stab of sympathy, that this was what it must look like when someone went mad. Krampus stepped down into the clearing, and Julian's eyes bulged so far Alex thought they really might pop right out of his head.

"I-I'll k-kill you too," Julian croaked. "I'll cut off your head and stick it on my wall."

Krampus raised a bristling eyebrow, and turned to Richard. "There are no bad children here," he said through gritted teeth.

"What?" cried Alex. "No, he's terrible! You can have him!"

All the colour drained from Julian's face as Richard sliced through the dressing gown belt ("Hey, that was new!" Isobel spluttered) with one swipe of the pocketknife.

"He's all yours," Richard said.

Krampus crouched. Julian whimpered. Krampus pounced. Julian staggered back. Krampus whirled, fangs bared and claws outstretched. Julian bolted, straight into the hole in the mountainside.

For a few seconds the cave echoed with the scrabbling of Krampus' hooves and Julian's horrified shrieking. But the sounds of the chase faded quickly, and soon Julians' screams were lost to the bowels of the mountain.

The hand was still in the clearing where Julian had kicked it. It was cold, and dirty, and looked as though it had been stepped on at least once, but when Alex bent to pick it up, he saw that it was mostly undamaged, except for the missing fingertip. He brushed off the worst of the dirt on his pants.

It was over. He wasn't sure how he knew, but he did. The second the last sounds of Krampus' hooves had been swallowed by the cave, it was as though the whole of Nowhere had exhaled a giant breath that none of them knew it had been holding. A chilly wind blew lightly through the trees, making the drifts of snowflakes dance on their way down to the ground. An owl hooted softly from somewhere above, and a rustling from in the woods sounded like squirrels or chipmunks at play. It was Christmas Eve; in just a few hours the sun would rise on Christmas Day. There would be presents, and carols, and great big meals of turkey and pork before everyone went out to play with their new toys. Most of the town would never know that two enemies had been defeated outside the Red House tonight.

Alex held out the hand to Carl, who took it and held it as though it were something precious – which, Alex supposed, it truly was.

"Merry Christmas," said Alex.

The children cheered.

<h1 style="text-align:center">18</h1>

Carl did his best to hold still as Maureen used her neat, precise whip stitch to attach his hand back to his arm. The open end of the wrist was redder than when it had arrived, the grapefruit pink of the exposed inside deepening towards red. But Carl assured her that the attachment would take, and sat with only the slightest of winces as the needle made its careful way in and out of the skin.

"Does it hurt?" Katharina asked sympathetically. Her own wrist was still tightly bundled in Alex's dad's tie.

Carl shook his head. "Not really," he said. "But it does feel weird. It never stops feeling weird."

He flexed his fingers carefully, and Maureen shot him a look of disapproval. Everyone fell silent for a few minutes while Maureen finished up the wrist, then stitched the open end of the little finger into a neat, closed seam.

"There," she said, sitting back and admiring her handiwork. Carl moved his fingers one by one; he stretched them out, then made a fist. The seam pulled a little as he rotated his hand, but it held.

He looked around at the Liars. "Thanks," he said. He laughed a little, and shook his head. "I mean, *thanks*," he said. "I don't know how to…"

He cleared his throat. "You found me. You put me back together. You *fought* for me."

"Correction," interrupted Joe. "We kicked Krampus' butt for you."

Everyone laughed at that.

Carl blushed deeply. "Yeah," he said, "you did. I don't think I can ever pay you back for that."

He went quiet again. Alex looked at him, sitting on his upturned crate, flexing his hand gently back and forth. There was something about him that seemed different now, in the early hours of the morning with pale winter light straining to clear the horizon.

Carl shivered, and reached for the shirt he had draped over a nearby crate, and Alex suddenly realised what it was. Carl looked *normal*. Even with his pointed ears and upturned nose; even with the whisper-thin lines tracing across his body where the Liars had stitched him back together, there was something about Carl that suddenly looked real, and human, and like just another twelve-year-old boy. Alex felt a sudden, unexpected wave of sadness for him. After going through so much, and travelling so far…he was still just a boy.

"What'll you do now?" Richard asked, breaking the heavy silence.

Carl shrugged as he buttoned the shirt, his

newly-attached hand still a little clumsy with the buttons. "I don't know," he said. "No point going back to Calistoga. Probably no one I knew is even there any more. I wanted to go to San Francisco once upon a time, but..."

He trailed off, with a sad little smile. "A life of adventure doesn't seem so appealing any more, you know?"

"So stay here in Nowhere," Maureen said. Everyone turned to look at her. "What?" she asked.

"I...I don't know," Carl said. "I don't know anyone here..."

"You know us," Richard said pointedly.

"...and I don't have any family..."

"Neither do I," said Joe.

"And what if I don't fit in?"

"It's not so bad," Katharina and Maureen said simultaneously.

Carl thought about it, and Alex thought he saw something like hope kindle in his big brown eyes. They didn't really have a plan – no idea where Carl would stay, no clue how to enrol him in school, no sense of what a future in Nowhere would look like for him. Yet somehow, Alex felt a sense of rightness make its way around the room, from him to Joe to Maureen to Katharina to Richard, and all the way to Carl on his upturned crate with his half-buttoned shirt. He could be one of them; all they had to do was make it so.

Carl looked up at Alex, his brown eyes brimming. "And what do I do if people ask me where I'm from?" he asked.

Alex grinned. "Easy," he said. "You lie."

Excerpt from *Second Impressions*

1978

1

The phone rang, and Sami Pyreneesi thought long and hard about whether she wanted to answer it.

There was the phone call she wanted to get, the one she hoped for every time she heard that shrill alarm, and that she came away from feeling leaden every time she did not get it. There was the phone call she dreaded, the one she hadn't had to face yet but was sure was coming every time the ringer cut through the house like a siren. And then there were all the other calls, the appointments and social calls, the family members checking in, the telemarketers and wrong numbers and pollsters and reminders from the library that she still had books overdue. Every call, neither the one she wanted nor the one she dreaded, was a little stab to the chest, a yes, no, thankyou, I'll get those books back soon, ma'am, all while she swallowed back the urge to scream at whatever poor soul was on the other end of the line: *didn't they know she was waiting for an important call!*

And when the call was done and the phone back in its cradle on the wall, she would wish it could have gone on a little bit longer: just a normal call on a normal day, like any other woman in Nowhere might get.

Sami considered just letting it ring. She had done that a few times, just so people wouldn't think she spent the entire day at home, waiting for the phone. And she didn't, really: she went out shopping, and to the library, to borrow romance novels she kept forgetting to return, and even sometimes to visit with friends. It shouldn't matter that the visits were short (barely a cup of coffee), or the shopping trips hurried (two pounds of ground beef and a bag of tomatoes, thank you), or that she called ahead to the library so she wouldn't have to spend time hunting down her books (any three from Harlequin, not the historicals). She went out. She lived a little.

The sound of the phone was like nails on a blackboard. She couldn't let it keep ringing. It would split her head right in two if she let it. Sami got up out of her chair, smoothed down the front of her blouse, and answered the phone.

"Mrs Pyreneesi?" said the voice on the other end. "We've found your son."

Sami felt her breath hitch as her brain sprinted through the possibilities.

He's with a Mormon family in Geyserville, and they've decided to adopt him.

He hopped a train to LA, and now he's in the pictures.

A mystery great-uncle died and left him a lot of money, and he's bought a castle in Europe.

The one thing she refused to think was, *He's here at the station and we're bringing him home.*

But that, of course, was what the voice on the other end said.

Sami would never have admitted, even to herself, that she did not want Elliot to come home. She didn't want harm to come to him, of course. He was her son. Even when he was in trouble at school, even when she caught him with blood under his nails and toys that weren't his own, even when he screamed and punched the walls and said hateful things to her, he was her son. She didn't want to think of him cold and still in a ditch, or half-sunk in the waters of the lake.

But did he have to come home?

Elliot had been missing for thirteen days. It had started, as it so often did, on a Friday afternoon after school. Elliot's friends had wanted to drive to Santa Mira to see a movie. Sami hated the way they drove, and besides: she had made pork chops for dinner. They had fought; they had both said cruel things; and someone had thrown a plate (probably Elliot – in fact, definitely Elliot; she could still feel the little ache on her chin where the plate had shattered and cut a slice in it). Elliot had grabbed his boots and his rain-slicker, and stormed out into the sleet.

Sami hadn't bothered to call his father. Elliot stormed out all the time; there was no point kicking up a fuss.

That night she had called around his friends' mothers, to see whether Elliot was staying the night with someone. No, they all said, no Elliot here. Besides, Lon/David/Micah/Jasper is grounded and can't have friends over, so if Elliot were here we'd send him right home.

It seemed like most of Elliot's friends were grounded every other week.

That still hadn't been enough to worry about. Sometimes, when he was mad, Elliot went out and spent the night in his treehouse, flicking through his magazines and listening to the radio. Sami had tried going out there a few times before, with peace offerings of pop and cookies, but it always ended with Elliot pelting her with acorns and paperclips and whatever else he had stashed up there. If he didn't feel like staying in the treehouse, sometimes Elliot would hike all the way to the property line, where an old outbuilding with a woodburning stove was a decent enough place to stay the night if you were in a mood and wanted some space.

Sometimes, Sami suspected, Elliot gathered up his friends to go spend the night in the caves, where the roots of Mount Konocti opened to the world and little caverns in the rock offered a taste of adventure before deepening into an endless, directionless labyrinth. Sami hated to think of Elliot going to the caves alone, or even with his friends, but she knew that the worst way to keep him away from them was to tell him not to go. So she chewed on the inside of her cheek, and hoped – not trusted – that Elliot and his crew were smart enough to stay in the parts of the caves where you could still see the sky.

Maybe there was a girl, Sami thought in those first couple of days. Maybe Elliot's sweet on someone and wants to steal time with her, away from the grownups, away from the admonitions about staying safe, away from the whole world if they had to. That must be it. Elliot's in love, and has lost track of the time.

But Sami knew most of the girls at Elliot's school, since she taught a sewing class there twice a week. And she knew a lot of the other girls too, the ones who were homeschooled or sent away or had dropped out to help out at home. They all did the same thing whenever she mentioned her son: they didn't say anything, but they curled their lips and shrugged their shoulders and showed her, plain as day, that they'd rather be dead in a ditch than go out with Elliot Pyreneesi.

It wasn't until the fourth day – a Tuesday, so he'd already missed a day of school – that Sami considered that something might have happened to her son.

Her husband was no help at all. Around the

time Elliot had turned ten (in fact, right around the time his moods had really started), Sal Pyreneesi had decided to take on a second job doing short-haul deliveries around Lake County. The extra money was more than nice: it had paid for an extension to the house and doubled Sami's allowance for books and other enjoyments, but it meant that Sal really didn't know what went on around the house at all. He saw his son for an hour in the evening, if he was lucky; sometimes he was home on weekends, but then Elliot was usually out, doing whatever he did with his friends and usually causing at least one frantic call home to come clean up some mess he'd made.

Sal wasn't home to get the phone calls after Elliot had gone missing. Sal had never had to tell a librarian an overdue book was less important than his runaway son. That was Sami's job: her punishment for reading romances instead of being a secretary or a paralegal or something else useful, she supposed.

It had been twenty minutes since the end of the phone call. The police station in Nowhere was only seven minutes away by car, eighteen on foot. If she didn't set out soon, she supposed the friendly old police chief who was keeping Elliot down there would wonder if she even really loved him.

Sometimes she wondered that herself.

About the Authors

Dani Colman is a writer and educator originally from London, England. She currently lives in San Francisco with her husband and two cats, and puts food on the table by teaching robots to hunt lawyers.

Phillip "Chase" Martin is a magician from Lake County, CA, which he describes (correctly) as the absolute middle of nowhere. He spends his days doing card tricks for his two cats, who will someday learn to appreciate it.

Christmas in Nowhere:

A Nowhere, CA Christmas Collection

Collects all three Nowhere, CA Christmas Specials, plus an exclusive new story.

Available on amazon.com at
https://www.amazon.com/dp/B08NHBQK6N

www.ingramcontent.com/pod-product-compliance
Lightning Source LLC
Chambersburg PA
CBHW020956160726
47994CB00006B/2254